MW01488752

*A Forever Kind of Love*

# A FOREVER
# Kind of Love

## LYNNE LORING

*AVALON BOOKS*
THOMAS BOUREGY AND COMPANY, INC.
401 LAFAYETTE STREET
NEW YORK, NEW YORK 10003

PRINTED IN THE UNITED STATES OF AMERICA
ON ACID-FREE PAPER
BY HADDON CRAFTSMEN, SCRANTON, PENNSYLVANIA

To my daughter, Cindy,
who so cheerfully indulges me in my efforts to be a mother.

## Chapter One

"I promised you a rose garden, and here it is," Connie D'Angelo said as she opened the gate to a small, fenced courtyard near a side entrance to City Medical Center.

Rob Nelson, the teenage boy who walked beside her, balanced cautiously on his new and unfamiliar metal crutches as he followed her into the little garden. Absorbed in his painstaking task, he barely glanced at the beds of lush spring greenery that bordered the walkway. "This is nice, but where are the roses?"

"They're not in bloom yet. You're supposed to use your imagination." Connie watched her patient closely as he maneuvered his way along the sidewalks that crisscrossed the courtyard. Although she offered him

1

no support, she moved close beside him, ready to offer her help if it should be needed.

He wobbled precariously as he supported his weight on the crutches, gingerly guarding the leg that was encased in a plaster cast. "This place at least beats the dungeon," he said.

"If you're referring to the exercise room where I perform my life's work, I resent that description," Connie replied with feigned indignation. "I'll have you know that the physical-therapy department at City Medical Center is one of the best equipped in the country, and we take great pride in the cheerful, loving care we offer our patients."

Rob grinned. "All that's lacking are the bullwhips."

"What an uncharitable thing to say about us overworked, unappreciated physical therapists who daily bend our backs to make life more meaningful for others. However, I thank you for your suggestion, and I'll bring it up at the next staff meeting."

This good-natured banter was a part of Rob's physical-therapy sessions. The lighthearted eighth-grade student had injured a knee in a school basketball game and, after corrective surgery, was undergoing rehabilitative therapy as an outpatient at the hospital. Connie, as a part of her job in Rehabilitation Services, was the physical therapist assigned to his case.

Cheerful, confident Connie was particularly effective with teenage boys, who were always looking for shortcuts on the path to recovery. Her casual yet sensitive approach inspired their trust and good will, but she was firm in refusing to accept excuses in place of the hard work successful therapy required.

Rob had been an especially cooperative patient, and she had decided to reward him by moving his treatment session outdoors. It was a sunny afternoon in early April, too pretty a day for a student who had been in class all day to be confined indoors.

The little garden, which was tucked away in a recess of the building outside the physical-therapy department, provided a perfect setting for outdoor treatment sessions. It was a pleasant retreat where patients could practice climbing steps and negotiating curbs and sidewalks. Screened by tall hedges and guarded by a high, wrought-iron gate, it offered privacy and safety from the jostling streams of people passing through the busy corridors of the hospital.

Connie watched with satisfaction as Rob made his way along the path through the garden. He was quickly gaining confidence in his crutches. ''I think you're just about ready to storm the halls at school,'' she announced after he successfully mastered the three steps to a lower terrace of the garden. She pointed to a bench angled in a shady corner. ''For the moment, however, you've earned a rest.''

As they approached the bench, she saw that it was occupied. A man was stretched out upon it, a newspaper covering his face to shield it from the late-afternoon sun. Apparently he was enjoying a nap. She frowned. The garden was for the use of the patients, not the public. Certainly not, from the looks of him, vagrants like the man who was asleep on the bench.

She strode to the bench and lifted the newspaper from the man's face. "Excuse me," she said authoritatively. "You can't sleep here."

The man's eyes flew open. He sat up, startled, trying to shake off his confusion. He ran a hand through tousled, collar-length blond hair as his blue eyes focused blearily upon her. "I'm sorry. I must have dozed off."

She regarded him with disfavor. "This isn't a public place, you know. I'm afraid you'll have to go somewhere else."

In spite of her stern remarks, Connie felt a twinge of sympathy. The man was young, probably no older than thirty, dressed shabbily in torn jeans and a frayed denim jacket. Obviously he was a street person in need of a place to rest. It was sad to see a person so young having already fallen on bad times.

Still, her duty was to her patients, and the facilities had to be protected from strangers who wandered onto the hospital grounds. "If you're in need of a place to rest, I can direct you to a shelter," she suggested. "But you can't stay here."

"It's okay, Miss D'Angelo," Rob called out as he came up behind her. "He's not a bum. He's with me."

Connie shot a skeptical glance at Rob. "Then what's he doing here?"

"He's waiting for me. He brought me to the hospital for my therapy. He's a teacher at my school."

She regarded the stranger on the bench dubiously. What kind of teacher was this?

The man gave her a sleepy smile. "Sorry if I wandered into the wrong stall. I was waiting for Rob, and the garden looked inviting, so I came in and sat down. Next thing I knew, I was being evicted."

"I don't want to seem rude, but the garden really is intended for the use of the patients. It's a place where they can work on outdoor skills in privacy," Connie said.

He stretched lazily, reminding her of a sleek cat. Then, pulling himself to his feet with obvious reluctance, he held out his hand. "I take it you're Miss D'Angelo, the physical therapist Rob has told me so much about. I'm Eric Lindstrom, his history teacher."

Connie tried to conceal her surprise. In his threadbare jeans and a paint-stained T-shirt, this man could surely not be a member of the teaching staff at the prestigious boys' school Rob attended.

Eric Lindstrom must have guessed her thoughts, because he said with an engaging smile, "I guess I don't look the part of a faculty member, but I tend to let up on the dress code in my off hours. The classroom jacket-and-tie bit rides a little heavy as a steady thing."

"I suppose," she said doubtfully. While she liked casual dress as well as the next person, this man's disreputable outfit went a shade too far. A teacher ought to set an at least minimally respectable example for his students. Still, it was Friday afternoon and school was out for the weekend. Certainly his choice of clothing during after-school hours was no business of hers.

She was about ready to accept the conciliatory handshake he offered when he turned his attention to his student. "You're handling those crutches like a veteran, Rob. I expect you'll be navigating the traffic in the school corridors anytime now."

Connie nodded in agreement. "A little more work on the steps, and he'll be ready, I think."

"What I'm wondering about is when I'll be ready to play basketball," Rob said with a trace of impatience.

"Sorry, but that's not my department," Connie answered. "You'll have to take it up with your doctor."

"You won't have to worry about basketball anytime soon, anyhow," Eric Lindstrom said. "It'll be at least six months before the season comes around again."

"I know, but I need to be practicing." Rob's expression revealed his first real sign of frustration.

"You'll get plenty of practice when you're ready. Your coach will see to it," his teacher promised. Dismissing the subject with an encouraging smile, he turned to leave. "Right now you've got practicing of another kind to do, so I'll get on my way and let you do it. I'll meet you in the lounge at the physical-therapy department when you've finished."

"You're welcome to stay here with us if you like," Connie said.

He shook his head. "I'd be a distraction. Besides, I can use the time to do some work that I brought along with me." There was a distinct hint of humor in his eyes as he added, "It's been nice meeting you, Miss D'Angelo. I look forward to seeing you again, now that I'm properly accredited."

He set off down the walk then, leaving them to their work. Connie watched him until he rounded the tall hedge that bordered the garden and disappeared from sight. Observing his tall, lithe figure and self-confident carriage, she was very curious about him. What a contradictory man he was, she thought.

The rest of the session went without incident, and Connie was well satisfied with Rob's progress by the time they left the garden. His athletic strength and agility were proving to be of great help to him in mastering the art of the crutches he would be using for the next few weeks.

As he had promised, Eric Lindstrom was waiting in the visitors' lounge at the PT department when Rob was ready to leave. He was talking to one of the other staff members when Rob and Connie joined him. Perhaps her earlier lack of cordiality had put him off, because he spoke only a few polite words to her before he promptly departed with Rob.

"Wow," said Gena Farrell, the staff member with

whom he had visited. "Now there's a man to brighten your day. Who was that gorgeous hunk, anyhow?"

Connie had to agree that, with his thick blond hair, vivid blue eyes, and appealing smile, Eric Lindstrom was indeed an eye-catching man. "He's a teacher at the boys' school Rob attends," she explained. "He brought Rob in for his therapy today."

"What a shame to waste him on a boys' school! Can't you just imagine how ecstatic a bunch of teenage girls would be to have a teacher who looks like that?"

"That's probably why he's teaching teenage boys."

"I suppose. There sure weren't any like him around at my school."

"Nor mine," Connie admitted.

"For that matter, we don't get many guys like him around here, either," Gena said with a wistful sigh. "If he brings Rob in again, let me know. I'd love to get better acquainted with him."

"Don't get your hopes up," Connie warned. She had to smile at exuberant Gena, who was forever on the lookout for an attractive male. "For all you know, he's got a wife and a houseful of kids."

Gena shook her head. "Not him. I can always tell a single man. They have a free, unshackled look about them."

"He's a free soul, for sure. I'd say from the short conversation I had with him that he's a real one-of-a-kind sort of guy." Connie shrugged, dismissing thoughts of Eric Lindstrom. He definitely wasn't her type. She had the feeling he was the disruptive sort of man who could create havoc in a staid, placid, orderly life.

Thinking of orderly lives, she hurried to attend to the day's few remaining duties. Having finished with her last appointment, it was time to move on to her own structured personal life. On Friday nights the entire D'Angelo family congregated at her parents' home, and her mother would be counting on her help with the family dinner. After she drove home through the heavy evening traffic, there would still be an evening's work ahead of her.

The traffic in and out of the hospital was always hectic on Friday evening, what with people hurrying to their weekend activities. As Connie drove from the hospital parking lot, she made a daring turn into the long line of vehicles that sped past, wedging her small black compact car into a tiny space between a heavy van and a pickup truck.

She had traveled only a few blocks when the engine of her car suddenly began to miss. After a few feeble surges it sputtered and died. She managed to steer it to the curb, but although she tried frantically to coax it into action, it refused to start.

To a chorus of honking horns from the cars trapped behind her, she got out of her stalled car and raised its hood. Ignoring the irritated drivers as they maneuvered around her, she peered down at the unresponsive engine. Although she had little expectation of finding the cause of its failure in the maze of hoses and wires, she felt obliged to at least make the effort.

As one vehicle after another whizzed past without an offer of help, she tried to decide what she should do. While she disliked the thought of leaving her stalled car to the mercy of the heavy evening traffic, she had no option but to find a telephone and call home. Her brother, Frankie, should be getting in from work before long, and her mother could send him to help her.

She had turned on the emergency flashers and was locking the car door when a small blue van stopped behind her. The driver climbed out and came toward her. "It looks like you've got trouble. Can I give you a hand?" he called out as he approached.

If his blond hair hadn't identified Eric Lindstrom, his frayed jeans and denim jacket would have been instantly recognizable. Connie turned to him in relief. "I doubt that there's anything to be done for the car, but I'd really appreciate it if you could make a telephone call for me."

He walked to the front of the car and looked at the engine. Connie stood beside him, watching him wiggle some wires. "Not that I'd know what to do if I could find anything wrong," he said with an apologetic grin. "I'm sorry to say I'm not much of a mechanic. Since I'm sure you've done all you can to start it, all I can suggest is that we call in the experts."

"I'm afraid it's going to have to be towed to a garage," Connie agreed. "I was going to telephone my brother to come and help me. If you wouldn't mind stopping somewhere and making the call for me, I certainly would appreciate it.''

''I can do better than that. I have a car phone.'' He pointed to his van with a hint of pride. ''I may not be of any help with engines, but I can offer you the latest in communication.''

Connie accepted the offer gratefully. Within minutes she had contacted her brother. ''Frankie will be here in a little while,'' she reported. ''He says not to call a tow truck until he checks out my car.''

''Then I'll stay with you until he gets here.'' Eric leaned into the back part of the van and lifted out a Styrofoam cooler. ''I can even offer you something to drink while we wait for him.''

Connie selected a can of soda from the cooler, and they sat down on the grassy strip beside the curb to enjoy their drinks. ''Do you always carry iced drinks with you?'' she asked.

''Only when I think of it. Today I had loaded up to drive to the country after classes, but Rob turned up without transportation to the hospital for his therapy. There was a family emergency and his mother couldn't drive him, so I volunteered. I had forgotten about the sodas in the cooler until now.''

''I'm glad you remembered them,'' Connie said after drinking thirstily. ''And very lucky that you were still near enough to the hospital to pass by.''

''I've been waiting all this time at the hospital with

Rob. His father was to pick him up after his therapy but was delayed in getting there. I had just left them and started home. I recognized you standing beside your car and thought maybe you could use some help.''

"This turned out to be your day for good deeds, didn't it? It was very good of you to forgo your trip to the country.''

"I didn't mind. I know how important Rob's therapy is.''

Connie nodded. "Proper therapy can make a lot of difference in how complete a recovery a patient gets.''

"I know. I've got the thumb to prove it.''

He held up his left hand for her inspection. She exclaimed at the sight of it. The first joint of the thumb was knobby and enlarged and protruded to one side at a grotesque angle.

She took his hand in hers and bent over it to examine the misaligned finger. "How in the world did you manage to do this to yourself?''

"I dislocated it when I was a kid and didn't take proper care of it. I liked sports in school, and the thumb kept getting reinjured, eventually ending up the way it is. Fortunately, it doesn't bother me, but it isn't a pretty sight.''

She bent over the thumb for a critical inspection, gently probing and massaging it with deft fingertips. "It isn't too late, you know. An orthopedist might still be able to correct this. It could involve some surgery, of course, to realign the joint.''

"Ouch. Thanks for the tip, but I'm satisfied with my poor thumb the way it is."

"You could have joint problems later on," she warned.

"I'll take my chances. It happens that I faint at the sight of a surgical knife. Physical therapy is another matter, however," he said as she continued manipulating his thumb. "What you're doing there feels pretty good."

Connie glanced up to see him looking at her with a satisfied smile. She became aware that their heads were only inches apart and that she was holding hands with a total stranger. A unique sort of stranger who was becoming more of an enigma by the moment.

Reacting instinctively, she drew away from him. As she dropped his hand, she heard a voice call out from behind her. Turning, she saw a dark-haired young man who bore a marked resemblance to her approaching them. Her brother Frankie had arrived.

At her first glance at him, she could tell that Frankie was displeased. "This is Eric Lindstrom," she explained, scrambling to her feet. "He stopped to help me."

Frankie brushed aside the introduction. "We'd better see what can be done to get your car out of this traffic before someone rams into it. Have you tried to start it?"

"It doesn't do anything, Frankie. I didn't want to keep trying to start it for fear I'd run the battery down."

"In other words, you haven't tried anymore. The engine could just have been flooded, you know," he grumbled. He strode toward the car impatiently and slid into the driver's seat. After several futile attempts to start the engine, he went to the front of the car and bent down to look beneath the hood.

Connie followed behind him, offering explanations. "The engine just quit and wouldn't start again. The same way it did last time."

"The alternator is probably acting up again. I told you this car was no good. It was a lemon when you bought it." Frankie raised up from his inspection of the engine, closed the hood of the car, and brushed the grime from his hands. "There's nothing to do but have it towed in. I'll have to find a phone and call a garage."

"Eric has a phone in his car. I'm sure he won't mind if we use it." Connie cast a questioning glance at Eric.

"Sure. I'll be glad to help in any way I can." Eric led the way to his van and opened the door. Frankie accepted the use of the telephone without thanks.

While he telephoned the garage, Connie and Eric waited beside the van. "I probably should have called the garage myself, but Frankie wants me to call him when I have car trouble. He's good with cars, you see." Embarrassed by her brother's brusque attitude, she felt called upon to explain it to Eric.

"It's always hard to decide what to do when your car breaks down," he sympathized.

"Especially when you know as little about cars as

I do. Even though this is supposed to be the day of independent women, engines are still a mystery to me.''

''I know what you mean. As you observed, they're not my strong point, either. I accept my shortcomings, though. All of us can't be all things.''

She was ready to suggest that he try to convince her brother of that fact when Frankie climbed out of the van and joined them. ''They're sending out a tow truck to take care your car. We can leave it here and go home.''

While Connie locked her car, Frankie offered Eric a perfunctory nod and started toward his own car, which he had parked behind the van. She lingered to offer her thanks for Eric's help.

''No problem,'' he assured her. ''I just hope there's nothing seriously wrong with your car.''

Frankie, who had already climbed into his car and started the engine, called out impatiently, ''We've got to get going, Connie. Mom needs you at home. She freaked out when she found out you were going to be late. Her back is acting up again today.''

Connie climbed into the car beside her brother. As he drove away, he continued his complaints. ''You've got to smarten up about your car. You ignore it until it breaks down, and then you don't know what to do.''

''You're the one who told me not to call the garage,'' she reminded him.

''The thing is, you always pick the worst times to

bug out. You know how Mom is on Fridays when the whole family is coming to dinner. Besides, she worries about you being stranded on a street corner.'' He shot a disapproving glance at her. ''It's a good thing she didn't see that guy you picked up. Who was he anyway?''

''He brought a patient in for therapy this afternoon.''

''The two of you looked pretty thick to me. What were you doing holding hands with him?''

''I was examining his thumb. He has a lot of displacement in the joint.''

''That's not your problem. He needs to see a doctor.''

''That's what I told him. Anyway, when he passed me on his way home from the hospital, he recognized me and stopped to help.''

''You wouldn't have needed help if you took proper care of your car,'' Frankie said grudgingly.

Connie sighed, tuning out her brother's criticism. She was used to it. For that matter, she had two more older brothers who were just as quick with advice. As the youngest child in her family and the only girl, she had grown up with brothers telling her what to do. She understood that their concern was well meant and had learned to accept it.

Listening to Frankie now, though, her enthusiasm for the coming family gathering faded. The gloomy prospect of going home to hungry brothers and sisters-in-law, boisterous nieces and nephews, Pop's lectures about cars and Mama's aching back suddenly had little appeal. She loved her family, and she tried to be a good daughter, but she wanted something more out of life. As much as she liked her work and as much as she enjoyed her family, she wanted more than the uneventful future that stretched ahead of her.

Oddly, the thought evoked the memory of Eric Lindstrom napping happily in the sunshine in the hospital garden, unconcerned and unfettered by proprieties. Strange, unconventional man that he was, he had been the bright spot in her day.

## Chapter Two

B y the time Connie and Frankie arrived home, the D'Angelo house was crowded with family members, all of whom were hungry. Connie brushed aside her mother's anxious questions and hurried upstairs to change clothes before she prepared dinner.

Usually, after a day's work, she took time to shower away the hospital grime. Tonight she settled for a thorough washing of her hands and a change into jeans and a comfortable pullover. Dinner was at best going to be late, and Pop D'Angelo was never in the best temper when he had to wait for his evening meal.

While Connie chopped vegetables for a salad and started chicken frying in an iron skillet, she heated a large kettle of water in which to cook the pasta. In the D'Angelo household, pasta always accompanied any other dishes that might be served at the main meal. The pasta sauce, taken from the freezer, simmered on the stove. As Connie worked, she listened with half an ear to her mother's lamentations.

"It's that car. It won't run, and you've got no business being stranded on street corners with a broken-down car. It's dangerous," Stella D'Angelo protested as she sat at the large, round kitchen table watching her daughter.

"I'm careful, Mama. Besides, it's only happened a couple of times before."

Stella groaned as she leaned against the pillow that padded the back of her chair. "I don't see why you have to work at the hospital, anyhow. Your father provides well for his family, and you don't need a job. There's plenty for you to do here at home."

"I like my work at the hospital, and I like having a job."

"Then work in your father's hardware store where you'll be safe. A big city is no place for a girl to go wandering around alone." Stella turned to her two daughters-in-law, who sat at the table beside her. "Isn't that right?"

Both of them nodded dutifully. Janice, the pretty wife of Vic, the middle of the three D'Angelo sons, occupied herself with the chubby baby she held in her lap. Milly, wife of the oldest D'Angelo brother, Joe, gave her attention to the three noisy children who played beneath the kitchen table.

Connie didn't contest her mother's old-fashioned ideas. Stella and Sam D'Angelo still followed the traditions that had guided their families for generations. They had built their lives around their children and provided a comfortable, secure home for them. If their overprotectiveness of their youngest child became overwhelming at times, Connie accepted it as a natural part of her role as their only daughter. She understood that their concern was prompted by their love for her.

She did at times regret having moved back into her parents' home. There had been a glorious period the previous year when she had shared an apartment with Amanda Summers, a social worker at the hospital. It had been a wonderful time of freedom to come and go as she liked, and she had enjoyed every minute of it. Not that she wanted to do anything her parents disapproved of. It was just that a twenty-four-year-old woman wanted her independence.

Unfortunately—and maybe mistakenly, she sometimes thought—she had given up the apartment when Amanda married Ross McKinnon, a neurosurgeon at City Medical Center. The apartment had been lonely after the special friendship she and Amanda had enjoyed, and there was nobody else she wanted to share it with. When at the same time her mother began suffering with a painful back and requested her daughter's help, Connie had moved back to the family home.

She couldn't deny that there were times when she regretted her decision. She missed the freedom she had cherished, and at times she felt suffocated by the restraints of being treated as a child by parents and older brothers. Although she loved her parents and accepted her obligation to them, she often longed to be back in her own little apartment, living as she chose.

Tonight was one of the times. Maybe it was Frankie's bad temper while he was driving her home. Frankie was still single and, though four years older than Connie, also lived at the D'Angelo house. Of course, being a son, he came and went as he pleased, but maybe he, too, grew impatient with their parents' restraints. Perhaps he, like Connie, longed for a place of his own and a life apart from the family.

It was a guilty thought, which she put promptly out of her mind. Mama had worked hard for her family and had a right to ask her daughter for help now that she was getting older and her body was protesting its long years of service. It would have been ungrateful and mean-spirited to refuse her.

Connie was jogged from her thoughts when Milly's two older children came to the kitchen with a warning that Pop D'Angelo was getting impatient for his dinner. Hurrying to slide foil-wrapped loaves of bread into the oven, she put vegetables in the microwave oven to steam. This convenience was a concession from Stella, who refused to use it, fearing its invisible rays. Only Connie's refusal to cook without it had finally forced her mother's surrender.

In minutes the food was ready. Janice handed the

baby to her mother-in-law to hold while she set the dining-room table. Milly enlisted the help of her two older children in carrying the bowls of food to the dining room. Connie sent one of the younger ones to announce dinner to the D'Angelo men.

Sam D'Angelo presided at the head of the long table, his three sons seated to his right, Milly and the three older grandchildren to his left. Stella took her place at the foot of the table, flanked on one side by Janice and the baby and on the other by Connie and the two younger grandchildren.

Connie slid last into her place, which was positioned conveniently near the kitchen. While the women attended to the needs of the children, the men, led by Sam, carried on a spirited conversation. The talk, centering on business predictions and sporting events, did not turn to the women's interests until the dessert had been served.

Inquiring first of the grandchildren for reports of their week at school, Sam leaned back in his chair and looked down the table at Connie. "Frankie's been telling me about your car trouble. I've told him to start looking for a new one."

"I've got a friend who owns a dealership. He'll probably make me a good deal," Connie's oldest brother, Joe, spoke up.

Sam nodded his approval. "See what he offers, and if it sounds good to you, Frankie can take Connie's car around and see what kind of a trade-in he can make.''

''But I don't want a new car, Pop,'' Connie objected, feeling a familiar surge of irritation. As usual, her father and brothers were making decisions for her without regard for her own preferences.

Her father frowned. ''It's not a question of what you want. It's a matter of good judgment. If you're going to be driving back and forth to the hospital, you need a dependable car.''

''There's nothing wrong with the one I've got. I've had trouble with it only a time or two.''

''That's not how it seems to me,'' Frankie interrupted. ''Every time I look up, I've got to go across town in heavy traffic to bail you out of trouble.''

Connie gave him an exasperated look. ''You don't have to come, you know. I'm perfectly able to take care of myself. I can call the garage as easily as you can.''

Sam shook his head. ''That's not the point. It's just not a good idea for a woman to be out alone depending on strangers.''

''Especially when you consider some of the strangers who are apt to come along.'' Frankie shot a meaningful glance at her, and she waited resignedly for him to bring up the subject of Eric Lindstrom. All she needed was a family discussion of the perils of taking up with strange men.

Sam, however, having dealt with the matter of Connie's car, moved on to a discussion with his two older sons of the pros and cons of selecting a new one. Frankie didn't return to the subject of strangers. She could tell by the glint of mischief in his eyes, though, that he hadn't gotten the last bit of mileage out of her misadventure.

Once dinner was finished, the family divided into groups again. The men gathered around the television set in the living room to watch a basketball game; the older children played video games in the dining room. The women, after they had put the kitchen in order, sat around the kitchen table drinking coffee and sharing tidbits of news while they looked after the younger children. The pattern they followed was the same every Friday evening, but it was a nonetheless pleasant routine. The D'Angelos were a close-knit family who enjoyed being together and depended upon one another for love and support. Connie was genuinely fond of her sisters-in-law, and she adored her lively, brown-eyed nieces and nephews.

Only Frankie broke the family routine tonight, to keep a date with his current girlfriend. He stopped by the kitchen on his way out of the house and drew Connie aside. "Be sure to save me a piece of pie from the hungry horde," he said.

She smiled at him. In spite of their squabbles, they enjoyed a close, affectionate relationship. "What's it worth to you?"

"Silence. Not a word about the guy who was coming on to you this afternoon."

"It wasn't like that, Frankie, and you know it," Connie whispered, glancing over her shoulder at her mother. Stella had a built-in antenna that picked up instantly on her two younger children's intentions.

Frankie arched an eyebrow mischievously. "I know exactly how it was. I recognized the interested look on the guy's face."

"All you saw was a man doing someone a favor."

"And that was why you were holding hands with him? What was going on with you two, anyhow?"

"I told you. I was examining his thumb. It had been improperly set years ago, and we were discussing the importance of physical therapy. Actually, we'd been talking about the boy he brought in for treatment at the hospital earlier."

"If you say so. But at least the guy has been warned not to get any funny ideas about you."

"You made that clear enough. The poor man stops to do a good deed, and for thanks he gets the heavy-handed big-brother routine."

"Just looking out for my sister."

"I can look after myself very nicely, thank you."

He grinned. "Save me the pie, and we'll talk about it tomorrow."

"I'll save you the pie, but the subject is closed," she said with a reproachful glance at him.

At least, she hoped it was. Somehow nothing ever

remained private in this family. Around here, your life was an open book. In her case, a very dull book, she thought dejectedly as she went back to the table to join her mother and sisters-in-law. You were in bad shape when a chance encounter with an attractive stranger was the only interesting thing that ever happened to you.

And a chance encounter was certainly all that her meeting with Eric Lindstrom had been. She'd likely never see him again. And even if she did, it would mean nothing. The man was definitely not her type.

The episode had almost been forgotten by the end of the following week. The replacement of a simple part had taken care of Connie's car trouble and calmed her parents' fears; nothing more had been seen of Eric Lindstrom. Connie didn't even have occasion to see Rob Nelson again. Having mastered the use of his crutches, he would need no more physical-therapy sessions for the present.

It was a surprise then, on the following Friday, when she heard someone call out to her as she was leaving the PT department at the end of the day. At first she didn't recognize the man who stood in the corridor just outside the door. Only when he spoke to her the second time did she realize that he was Eric Lindstrom.

Today he barely resembled the man she remembered from the week before. He wore dress slacks and an attractive pullover sweater; a conservative tie was knotted neatly beneath the buttoned-down collar of his shirt. His hair was shorter and tidily combed, and the leather briefcase he carried lent an even more scholarly air to his appearance. Except for his remarkably blue eyes, she wouldn't have recognized him as the carefree vagrant in threadbare jeans whom she had seen the previous week asleep on a park bench in the hospital garden.

Her face must have mirrored her surprise, because he smiled as he spoke to her a third time. "Apparently you don't remember me. I came in with Rob Nelson last week."

"Of course I remember you. You're also the nice man who stopped and helped me with my car." When a glint of humor appeared in his blue eyes, Connie decided there was no point in hiding her reaction to his changed appearance. "You do look a little different today, but mainly I'm surprised to see you here."

"I had business at the hospital and thought I'd stop by the PT department on the off chance that I might see you. I wanted to ask about your car."

"It's fine. It just needed a part replaced. I've been trying to tell the people at the garage that there has been something wrong with it ever since I got it. Of course, the mechanics never pay any attention to a woman's opinion about a car."

His lips curved in an amused smile. "We both seem to have our identity problem."

Connie wasn't entirely sure how to answer him. She settled for thanking him again for coming to her rescue.

"I was glad to be of help. To be perfectly honest, I enjoyed meeting you and stopped by in hopes that we might go somewhere and talk for a little while."

She hesitated. It was Friday again, dinner was waiting to be cooked, and there was no time to let her mother know she would be late getting home. Still, a woman had a right to a few minutes for herself, and this new Eric Lindstrom was a devastatingly attractive man. The family would survive if dinner was a little late for once.

"I can't take long, but I would enjoy something cool and refreshing before I do battle with the traffic," she said.

"I noticed a place across the street that looked promising—if you like frozen yogurt," Eric suggested.

A cold, creamy yogurt sounded heavenly to Connie after a long day at work, and the prospect of this intriguing man's company was even harder to resist. Deciding there were times when a woman owed something to herself, she put duty on the back burner and accompanied Eric with a clear conscience.

Seated at the snack bar across the street from the hospital, she sighed happily as she sampled a spoonful of strawberry yogurt. "How did you guess that this is one of my favorite treats and this little bar is one of my favorite places?"

"The same way I guessed you were going to choose

a strawberry yogurt, I suppose. You just look like that kind of person.''

''I wouldn't have picked you to be a vanilla-yogurt person. I'd have thought you'd choose something more exotic—pistachio, maybe, or caramel toffee.''

''It all depends on my frame of mind. Today I'm in my responsible, solid-citizen mode. I decided, after your reaction to me last week, that I needed to improve my image.''

''Your image wasn't all that bad, once I got past the ragged jacket.''

''Still, I'm not quite as far out as I appeared. I teach at the Rutherford School for Boys, have no bad habits, enjoy the best of health, and am sound of mind. I'm really quite a respectable guy.'' He leaned back in the booth and regarded her questioningly. ''I'm also very curious about you. So far, I know only that your name is Connie D'Angelo, you're a physical therapist, and you have a very protective older brother.''

''Actually there are three of them,'' Connie said with a wry smile. ''I'm the only girl in the family and the youngest child. So I get a lot of looking after. A good bit more, to be truthful, than I'd like.''

''It's understandable. And commendable. Brothers ought to look after their younger sisters. I know I would if I had one.''

''Have you any brothers?''

He shook his head. ''There are only my parents, and

they live in Florida. I get to see them often, though, during school breaks.''

''I understand, from what Rob Nelson tells me, that you teach history.''

''Among other things. I'm lucky enough to be able to pursue several interests.''

''Such as?''

''I'd just as soon talk about them another time. Right now I'm more interested in you. What about your interests, Connie? What do you like to do in your free time?'' He paused to spoon up the last of his yogurt while he considered the question. ''Or maybe I ought to be asking if you share your free time with someone special. I assumed you're not married, since Rob refers to you as Miss D'Angelo and you called on your brother for help instead of a husband. But maybe there's someone who might not like your being here with me.''

Connie shook her head vigorously. ''I don't answer to anyone. I'm definitely not married, nor am I anywhere close to it. I've got a good bit of living to do first.''

He nodded, pleased. ''In that case, maybe you'll consider going out with me sometime. Provided, of course, that I don't show up in ragged jeans.''

''As a matter of fact, I can think of places where those jeans might look just right,'' Connie said, smiling.

''That wasn't quite the kind of place I had in mind.

The one I was thinking of is a little different, though, and serves fantastic food. I think you'd like it.''

Connie was beginning to think she'd like going almost anywhere with Eric Lindstrom. His candid manner and appealing smile were having a remarkable effect on her. ''It sounds like fun,'' she said in decision. ''I'd like to try it.''

''Would there be a chance that you'd be free tomorrow night?'' he asked hopefully.

''There isn't a thing written on my calendar.''

''Then what do you say that I pick you up around seven and we take it from there?''

Connie hesitated. She dreaded the thought of Eric Lindstrom showing up at the house until she'd had time to lay the groundwork for his visit. Her male friends didn't find it really great at any time to be subjected to Pop and Mama's inquisition. And Frankie, considering his first impression of Eric, would be certain to disapprove of her going out with him. For a reason she didn't quite understand, this evening with Eric was important to her, and she was determined not to let her family spoil it for her. Making the decision to put her own wishes first, she suggested, ''Why don't I just meet you somewhere?''

For the briefest instant there was a quizzical expression in his eyes—maybe even a hint of disappointment. He only smiled, however, and said, ''I'll meet you wherever you say.''

They agreed that the hospital parking lot was as

convenient a meeting place as any. When Connie regretfully explained that she had to hurry home, he walked back to the hospital with her.

As she closed her car door, she asked in afterthought, "This place where we're going tomorrow night—what sort of thing should I wear to it?"

"Just wear what you'd wear to a place where you'd like to go."

"That tells me nothing about where we're going."

"That's the idea. It's a surprise."

He stood in the parking lot, watching Connie drive away. She drove home in happy anticipation. She had the feeling that wherever Eric Lindstrom took her, she was going to have a perfectly wonderful time.

## Chapter Three

It was with a sense of adventure that Connie dressed for her date with Eric on Saturday night. Half the fun of going out with him was trying to guess what kind of place he might choose.

He had said to wear something suitable for the sort of place she'd like to go, and she decided to take him at his word. She chose pleated pants and a matching cardigan sweater in a shade of pale moss green that complimented her short dark hair and lively brown eyes. The outfit was completed with a cream silk shirt accented by gold chains and an interesting leather belt. It wasn't a fancy costume, but then she didn't care very much for fancy places. And if her impression of Eric was in any way correct, he wouldn't be attracted to them, either. Still, who could guess what Eric might choose? That was the intriguing thing about him.

She took time before leaving the house to stop by the living room, where her parents were watching TV. Stella looked up from the crossword puzzle she was working. "You're dressed up," she observed. "What's going on tonight that's special?"

"Nothing special, Mama—just a Saturday-night dinner."

Her mother leveled an inquisitive glance at her, sensing with her unfailing intuitiveness that there was something different about the evening. "I hope you're not going to one of those places where strangers meet up and dance with each other."

Her remark captured Sam's attention, and he turned away from his television program to eye his daughter sternly. "She knows better than to go to places like that. Don't you, Connie?"

"I've got sense, Pop." Connie dropped a kiss on his forehead and began a quick retreat before her parents could think of any more pointed questions.

As she left the room, her mother was mumbling plaintively, "I don't see why the children can't be satisfied to stay at home and do something safe. I don't sleep a wink for worrying about what might happen to them." Connie smiled. For Stella, half the pleasure of motherhood was the excuse to worry.

She was almost out the back door when she passed

Frankie in the hallway. He eyed her appreciatively and whistled. ''You look great. Who's the hot date?''

''None of your business,'' she answered with a firm but affectionate grin.

''From the looks of the heavy war paint, maybe it ought to be,'' he teased.

''What's the big deal? Can't a girl put on some lipstick?''

''It's not the lipstick. It's the eyes. The way you've got them done up tonight, this guy is under siege.'' He looked at her curiously. ''Who is he?''

Connie parried the question by stepping back to inspect her handsome brother, who tonight was wearing a suit and tie. ''You're dressed for a pretty heavy evening yourself,'' she said. ''Who's the lucky girl?''

He chuckled. ''I get the message. I won't ask any questions if you don't. Just see that you stay out of trouble.''

''Don't I always?''

''Be sure you keep it that way.'' Although his admonition was spoken fondly, it held a meaningful edge.

Connie gave him a good-natured wave as she headed out the back door. She never really minded his brotherly concern. He had looked after her for as long as she could remember, and she had many times been grateful for the handsome older brother who was ready to come to her rescue. She regretted that she couldn't be open with him about her date with Eric, but she knew exactly what he would think of her plans, and she wasn't about to let his disapproval spoil the evening for her.

Eric was waiting for her at the hospital parking lot. She noticed at once that he was wearing a sport jacket and tie. "You're all dressed up," she commented as she joined him. "You and I seem to have had different ideas about where we'd be going."

"No way. I just came prepared for more than one eventuality. It'll be a pleasure to get rid of this." In a quick gesture he removed his tie and tossed it into the back of his van. Helping Connie onto the front seat, he closed the door ceremoniously behind her.

He gave her no hint of their destination as he drove off. She asked no questions, content to let him play out his surprise. When they bypassed the brightly lit downtown area of the city, however, and moved into an area of warehouses and loading docks, she became more curious by the moment. As well as a little dubious about this mysterious place he was taking her to.

He turned at last onto a street lined with old buildings that had been refurbished and converted to new use. The area extended for a couple of blocks and presented an inviting scene. Victorian storefronts had been restored and freshly painted. The lighted second-floor windows suggested the presence of studios and lofts. Quaint shops and restaurants were brightened by old-fashioned street lamps; a horse-drawn carriage clip-clopped its way through a neatly kept park at the end of the street. Here in a forgotten part of the city, this fascinating little enclave had been transformed into a charming restoration of the past.

"I had no idea there was anything like this here in town," Connie exclaimed in surprise.

"It's called Victorian Corner, and so far it's a well-kept secret. The restoration is being done by a group of artists and craftsmen who live as well as work here, and they would just as soon the area didn't get too well-known. They're more interested in living the way they want to than in making a lot of money," Eric explained.

"I don't think they'll be able to keep it to themselves much longer," Connie said, observing the throngs of sightseers who strolled among the shops.

He drove into a parking lot that was already filled with cars. He seemed pleased when Connie suggested a tour of the street. They spent a pleasant hour rummaging through studios and galleries, admiring artwork and sculpture, creations of stained glass and wood, handmade jewelry, leatherwork, and clothing. When he interrupted their sight-seeing so that they could move on to the restaurant where he had made their dinner reservation, she reluctantly left the fascinating displays.

The restaurant turned out to be as interesting as the shops. It was entered by a corridor lined with original artwork, and rambled through a series of small dining areas to a glass-enclosed atrium at the back of the building. They were seated at a table that overlooked a lantern-lit patio bordered by banks of shrubbery and equipped with wrought-iron furniture. Connie admired the lush greenery with surprise. It was hard to believe that this garden hideaway was tucked away amid the brick and concrete of the warehouses.

The food was an even greater treat. Each entree on the menu was a special chef's concoction. "You never know for sure what's going to be offered. The chef turns out whatever he's inspired to do," Eric explained.

Connie savored a mouth-watering taste of dilled salmon. "This food is fantastic—for that matter, so is the entire project. How did you happen to find out about it?"

"Some of the people who have opened shops here are friends of mine."

This individualistic enterprise was exactly the sort of undertaking she would have expected to attract the uninhibited man she had first met in the hospital court-yard. "I suppose you've been told that you really are a far-out kind of guy," she said.

"I'm not sure I know how to take that. If it means I'm some kind of dropout, I'm not at all. I'm gainfully employed in work I enjoy, I pay my taxes, and I obey the laws. Actually, I think of myself as quite a re-sponsible citizen."

"That's not what I meant. It's just that. . . ." She searched for words. "You seem so sure of what you want to do, and you're so very comfortable about doing it."

"Is that good or bad?"

"Good, of course. I admire people who know what they want and have the courage to go after it."

"You seem to be one of those people yourself. Apparently you like your work very much."

"I do like it. I like to feel that I'm helping people."

"You've certainly helped Rob Nelson. He's coming along very well after his knee surgery."

"He shouldn't have any problems if he follows through on his therapy, but proper rehabilitation is very important after the kind of injury he had."

"I can vouch for that. When I was in college, I had a knee injury similar to Rob's, and it put an end to my basketball career. Such as it was," Eric added with a wry smile.

"Wasn't your therapy successful?"

"There wasn't enough of it," he said regretfully. "The facilities were limited in the little town where my family lived at the time, and I was too impatient to return to play. As a result, I ended up with a knee that still gives me trouble from time to time."

"It's not too late for treatment," Connie suggested.

"That's a thought. The next time it rains and my knee acts up, I may just show up and ask you to test your skill on it. I might even throw in my crooked thumb." With a teasing smile, he held up his hand to display the abused finger.

Connie regarded the thumb doubtfully. "I'd do my best with the knee, but I can't make any promises about

the thumb. What in the world happened to it, anyhow?''

''I tangled with the wrong guy in an ice-hockey game
and discovered that a hockey stick can be a lethal
weapon.''

Connie couldn't help smiling at his rueful expression. ''Your adventures in childhood athletics don't
appear to have turned out too well.''

''I've got my scars.''

''Kids won't always admit it when they're hurt,''
she said, thinking of her competitive brothers, who
were still ready to risk life and limb in any physical
contest.

''That's why it's up to their coaches to see that they
don't play when they shouldn't.''

He moved on to another subject then, but Connie
was aware that she had seen yet another facet of his
character. A character she was coming to admire. He
was a man who seemed to care about other people, but
he definitely wasn't concerned with proving anything
to other people about himself. The more she learned
about this interesting man, the better she liked him.

They spent a pleasant dinner hour, exchanging stories and ideas. As they left the restaurant, Connie took
time to look at the original artwork displayed in the
foyer. There were paintings and drawings of all kinds,
one of which caught her attention at once. It was a
pen-and-ink sketch of a popular cartoon character fea-

tured in a weekly comic strip that appeared in the local newspaper.

"Look. There's Lindy," she said, leaning closer to inspect the drawing. Lindy was an offbeat little character who expressed the frustrations of an ordinary man trying to cope with present-day, fast-paced society. His philosophy struck a responsive chord in many younger people, and Connie tried never to miss the weekly strip. She turned excitedly to Eric. "This looks like an original. Do you suppose it was done by the real cartoonist?"

"If it's here, it's an original," he said.

She admired the drawing a moment longer. "Lindy is my absolute favorite cartoon character. He thinks like I do."

"I'm sure the cartoonist would be pleased to know that. Some people don't think much of Lindy's point of view."

"My father is one of them," Connie admitted. "He thinks ideas like Lindy's are going to bring society tumbling down around us. I'm sorry to say that Pop is being dragged kicking and screaming toward the twenty-first century."

Eric smiled. "Everybody has a right to his own ideas."

"Tell that to Pop. If you don't see it his way, you're a flaming anarchist."

"I'll try to remember that when I meet him," Eric said.

Connie judiciously dropped the subject, reminded of her problem in introducing him to her reactionary family.

They finished the evening with a stroll through the park and a ride in the horse-drawn carriage. Traveling down the quiet, lamplit street, Connie found a quiet harmony in Eric's company. She knew she would look back on this evening with him as a very special experience.

Eric seemed as reluctant as she to end the evening. When he took her back to her car at the hospital parking lot, he insisted on following her home. He didn't ask to be invited in but waited until she had parked her car in the driveway and was safely inside the house. She went to her room in an ecstatic frame of mind. The last thing he had said before he left her was to ask if he could see her again.

True to his word, Eric stopped by the PT department early in the week to ask Connie out for dinner. Soon they were seeing each other regularly. Every time she was with him, she enjoyed his company more, and he quickly became an important part of her life.

She had never before known a man quite like him. Their time together was a series of adventures. They went to a boat show, a baseball game, a concert, a foreign art film, a picnic in the park. They poked through art galleries, attended an opening performance of a local community theater, visited an estate sale where Eric bought an antique cuckoo clock.

It was a wonderful time of discovery. Eric proved to be a man of endless curiosity and limitless interests. He found small, hidden-away restaurants where they spent hours, sampling new foods and listening to ethnic music while they exchanged ideas and learned more about each other. Connie talked about her work, her concern for her patients, the sorrows and joys connected with the hospital; Eric spoke of his students, his commitments as a teacher, his fascination with the people he met on his excursions through the city.

For Connie, it was a period of enchantment, and the days sped past. The only cloud on her bright horizon was her family's increasing curiosity. Her parents complained of her frequent absences; her brother Frankie observed her comings and goings suspiciously. She knew that she couldn't delay much longer in introducing Eric to her family.

"You've got to face up to it, Connie. Your parents aren't going to be put off forever," Gena Farrell warned one day as they ate lunch together in the hospital cafeteria. Gena, who was the records supervisor for Rehabilitation Services, had become Connie's close friend and confidante during the months since she had come to work in the department.

"It's just that I don't know whether Eric is ready for my family. They've pretty overpowering," Connie said dubiously, unsettled by the very thought of subjecting him to her inquisitive parents.

"Your family may come on strong, but you can't keep them shut out forever. They know you're seeing someone, and they're going to demand to meet him, one way or another. The longer you put it off, the more difficult it's going to be for Eric." Having voiced her opinion, Gena gave her attention to the vegetable plate she had chosen for her lunch.

Connie poked at her salad dispiritedly. "You're right. I know you are. But it has all been so wonderful between Eric and me, and I don't want it to change. I'm afraid that once I bring my family into the picture, nothing will be the same."

"Isn't it really up to you and Eric to decide what you want your relationship to be? After all, you're a grown-up woman with a right to decide how you want to live your life."

"You don't know my family. Standing up to them is like standing in front of a steamroller. They just keep coming on until, next thing you know, you've been rolled over and flattened into the ground." Connie gave up the attempt to eat her salad and laid her fork down with a doleful sigh. "I'm used to them, but Eric can't be expected to put up with the kind of third degree he'll be in for."

"He might surprise you. He doesn't seem to be the kind of guy to let himself be pushed around. And if you're as important to him as it appears you are, he's not going to give you up without a fight.''

''But that's just the point. I don't want anybody to fight. I want them to like each other.''

''And maybe they will—in time, at least. In the meantime, you may have to decide how hard you're willing to fight for Eric.'' Gena took a sip of her iced tea and said with finality, ''I'll promise you that if I were lucky enough to have a gorgeous dreamboat of a guy like him in love with me, nobody would mess things up for me.''

''But maybe he's not in love with me,'' Connie said uncertainly.

''If he's not, he's giving an awfully good imitation of a man in love. And, if I can say so without getting you ticked off, you've got all the symptoms of a woman who is crazy about a guy.'' Gena leaned forward and eyed Connie earnestly. ''Admit it, Connie. Eric is a man to die for. You'll make a big mistake if you don't hang on to him.''

There was no questioning her sincerity. Strong-minded Gena, who believed in seizing life's opportunities and enjoying them to the fullest, would never let a possessive family stand in her way. ''You're right, of course,'' Connie admitted. ''Eric has become too important to me to let other people spoil things for us.''

''Then stand up to them. I know it isn't my place to give you advice, but I care enough about you to take a chance I'll make you mad at me. And, as your friend,

I have to say that you've done a pretty thorough job so far of letting your family manage your life. Don't let them do it this time. Don't let them interfere again.''

Connie went back to work weighing Gena's words thoughtfully. She knew her friend had given her sound advice, and she admitted that she had to face up to her problem. She owed it to Eric to explain her possessive family and let him decide for himself how he wanted to deal with them. Or, for that matter, whether he was willing to deal with them at all.

That night after work, when they met at a favorite restaurant for an early dinner, Connie gathered her courage and broached the subject to Eric.

''There's something I've been wanting to talk to you about,'' she began hesitantly. ''As you know, I've never gone out with you on Friday nights, and I'd like you to know why.''

He laid down his fork and gave her his full attention.

''It's my family, you see. Friday night at my house is the night when all the family gets together. There's a whole tribe of us—my two older brothers and their wives, and six grandchildren. And of course there's Frankie.''

''Most certainly, there's Frankie,'' he said with a dry smile.

Connie ignored the implication and plunged ahead. ''And there are my parents, of course. They're old-fashioned in their ways. Pop is. . . .''

When she faltered, he finished her sentence. "A man of strong ideas, I believe you've said."

She nodded. "And Mama is. . . ."

"A devoted mother who centers her life around her family and is fiercely protective of her only daughter and youngest child."

"I'm afraid so. The thing is that when everybody gets together, it's a real zoo. But I do want you to meet my family. That is, if you'd like to."

"As a matter of fact, I've been wondering when you were going to introduce me to them."

The understanding in his eyes told Connie that she hadn't needed to offer explanations. With his usual perceptiveness, he had already guessed the problem that lay ahead of them.

## Chapter Four

Friday turned out to be a difficult day. Connie's appointment schedule at the hospital was crowded, a staff meeting in the Rehab Department ran late, and traffic was unusually heavy after work. She arrived home, tired and tense, to find that her mother had made even fewer preparations for dinner than usual.

"I didn't know what you wanted. I'm not used to cooking for strangers," Stella complained, easing into her chair and massaging her back gingerly.

Connie was ready to remark that her mother wasn't used to doing much cooking at all anymore, but she cast aside the thought as uncharitable. Mama did what she could. She couldn't help it if her back kept hurting.

Unfortunately, the pain had worsened during the last twenty-four hours, the deterioration commencing when

48

Connie announced on Thursday that she was inviting a guest to Friday night's dinner. Stella had at once become hostile and suspicious. "It's a man, isn't it? The one you've been spending all your time with lately."

"Eric is a good person, Mama. He's taken me to lots of nice places, and it's my turn to entertain him. Besides, I wanted the family to meet him."

Stella had retreated into silence at the time. Now, reinforced by a day of fact-finding, she was ready with her objections. She sat at the kitchen table, nursing her sore back and voicing her disapproval while Connie began the dinner preparations.

"This Eric," she began. "Frankie says he knows him."

Connie's heart sank. Obviously, her brother had been talking to Mama, and it wasn't hard to guess what he'd had to say. "Frankie met him when my car broke down. Eric had stopped to help me."

"Frankie didn't think much of him."

"Frankie never thinks much of any of my friends." Silently Connie vowed to get even with her traitorous brother.

Stella persisted, unyielding. "Frankie says he's a bum."

"How would Frankie know?"

"He's a man. He knows these things about another man."

"I could bring Saint Peter to dinner, and Frankie would find fault with him," Connie retorted bitterly.

"Watch your mouth," Stella admonished. "You should listen to your brother. He's looking out for you."

"He's meddling in my life. And I don't like it." Connie dumped a bowl of chopped vegetables into the skillet in which she was making a sauce for the chicken that was baking in the oven.

"I don't see why you have to go looking for strangers to go out with, anyhow," Stella said mournfully. "There are lots of nice boys in families we know. Why can't you go out with some of them?"

"Because they're all still in high school and I'm twenty-four years old. Face it, Mama. I've grown up. I'm not a kid anymore."

Having made her pronouncement, Connie turned to the preparation of the food, cutting off the conversation with a loud banging of pots and pans and the whirring of the blender. Stella sat at the table, muttering to herself and shaking her head gloomily.

A few minutes later Vic and Janice D'Angelo arrived. Janice came into the kitchen carrying a crying baby and herding her two older children. "He's teething," she explained as she handed over her unhappy son for Stella to comfort. She turned her attention to the other two children, who were engaged in a noisy dispute over a toy.

Connie listened to the wailing baby and the squabbling children with dismay. The evening had started off exactly as she had feared it would, and she had the uncomfortable feeling that it wasn't going to get any better.

The family had assembled by the time Eric arrived. The doorbell could barely be heard over the din of contentious children, women's shrill voices, and the blaring television set. Connie hurried to the front door to greet him. There had been no time for her to brush her hair; her nose was shiny from the kitchen heat. She was tense from her harried dinner preparations and nervous about the coming evening.

In contrast, Eric looked calm and self-assured. He also looked unbelievably handsome, wearing a pullover sweater in a shade of blue that did incredible things to his eyes. His warm, reassuring smile was an instant comfort.

Conversation ceased when Connie led him into the living room and introduced him to her father and three brothers, who were intently watching a televised basketball game. Their greeting was polite but reserved. They remained sitting in a semicircle around the television set as Sam perfunctorily accepted Eric's offering of the customary gift of dinner wine, a brand that Connie had assured him was her father's favorite.

Continuing his introduction to the family, Connie led Eric to the kitchen. Sister-in-law Janice offered him a distracted but friendly greeting; Millie, after a quick inspection, smiled at him in guarded approval. Stella sat in stony silence, measuring him warily. Connie stifled an exasperated sigh. It was clear that her mother was determined to be difficult.

Returning to the living room with Eric, Connie hovered anxiously for a moment. Sam gestured to the chair beside him without turning his attention away from the basketball game. Her brothers, intent upon the game, didn't acknowledge Eric at all. Eric seemed unconcerned by the cool reception. With a reassuring smile at Connie, he took the chair beside Sam and gave his attention to the television set.

Connie returned to the kitchen to attend to the dinner. Her mother eyed her accusingly as she came into the room. Pointing a disapproving finger at the bottle of wine that Eric had set on the kitchen table, Stella complained, "I knew it. He's a drinker. Just look at the size of that bottle of wine he brought."

Connie turned her eyes heavenward. "For Pete's sake, Mama. He was only being polite. One small bottle wouldn't go around once in this crowd of people."

Stella shook her head, unconvinced. "That depends on how much a person expects to drink. What kind of people does he think we are?"

"Whatever he thought, it's a good brand of wine," Janice suggested with a grin, earning herself an admonishing glance from her mother-in-law.

Connie put an end to the conversation by loudly shuffling pots and pans as she resumed the dinner preparations. Stella retreated into an aggrieved silence. Janice judiciously busied herself with the cranky baby while Milly hurried to the dining room to set the table. As Connie ladled the food into serving plates, she could only hope fervently that things were going better in the living room for Eric than they were going for her in the kitchen.

When the dinner had been served and Connie slid into her place at the end of the table with the grandchildren, she perceived with dismay that the pattern for the evening had been set. Sam sat in his paternal seat of authority at the head of the table. Eric sat on his right, sandwiched between the two older D'Angelo brothers. Across the table, Frankie faced him with a noticeable lack of warmth.

Sam opened the conversation with a series of questions directed to Eric. Eric answered them affably, revealing that he was the only child in his family, that his father was a retired electronics engineer, that he was a teacher at the Rutherford School for Boys.

"Frankie says you teach history," Sam said.

"I teach one class in history, but mainly I teach art."

A silence fell over the table, broken only by the sound of four forks simultaneously hitting four plates. Four heads turned as Sam D'Angelo and his sons regarded Eric uncomfortably. In the D'Angelo family, artistic concerns were relegated to the women. Connie was as surprised at Eric's announcement as the male members of her family. While she had known of his interest in art, he had never mentioned his own involvement.

Sam regarded Eric uncertainly. "Are you saying you're one of those fellows who paints pictures?"

"I'm sorry to say that I'm not. I do a little bit with acrylics, but that's about it. The courses I teach give the students a foundation in graphic art."

Sam brightened. "Like in ads and signs?"

Eric nodded. "Sketching, drawing, illustrations— that sort of thing."

"These things you teach." Stella spoke up suddenly from the end of the table. "Do they show a man how to make a decent living?"

"Some men—and some women too—make a very good living with this kind of training," Eric replied.

Stella shook her head doubtfully. "It sounds risky to me, trying to make a living drawing pictures."

Eric laughed. "That's what my dad said when I told him what I wanted to study in college."

"Smart man," Stella muttered as, silenced by a warning glance from her husband, she turned her attention back to her dinner.

Sam moved the conversation to sporting events and local happenings. The three D'Angelo brothers joined in, seeming cheered by the change of subject. When dinner was over, Connie breathed a relieved sigh. As she was clearing the table, she glanced at Eric in an unspoken apology for the inquisition he had been subjected to. But the twinkle of amusement in his eyes told her he had survived her father's questioning unscathed.

When the family divided into their usual Friday-night groups, Eric declined Sam's invitation to join the men and watch the rest of the basketball game. "I'm going to earn my supper by giving Connie a hand with the dishes," he said. Seeming unaware of Sam's startled expression, he picked up the heavy tray of dishes that was ready to be carried to the kitchen.

After he had helped Connie clear away the dirty dishes and load them into the dishwasher, he insisted on washing the pots and pans while she dried and put them away. Working together, they took only minutes to put the kitchen in order.

"I was brought up to believe a man was a nuisance in a kitchen, but you're good at this," Connie told him as she hung the dishtowel on a rack to dry.

"I've had lots of practice. After all, I've had my own place for quite a while now."

"Do you mean you can cook?"

"A man's got to eat. As a matter of fact, I make an omelet that I'm quite proud of."

"I'm impressed," she said with admiring respect. "You know, you really are a surprising man."

"Maybe a little too surprising for your dad. I'm not making any points with him, hanging out here in the kitchen with the women, you know."

Connie giggled. "You picked up on it."

"Clearly. And in my own best interest I think I'd better get back to that basketball game."

On his way to join the men, he paused to speak to the women of the family, who were sitting in their customary places at the kitchen table, drinking coffee. As he turned to leave, he saw, standing just inside the kitchen door, a row of solemn-eyed D'Angelo grandchildren who were watching him curiously.

"Did I take your jobs away from you?" he asked them with a smile. "Are you disappointed because you didn't get to help your Aunt Connie with the dishes?"

They shook their heads, continuing to watch him steadily.

"Is there something you want to ask me?" he said to them at last. "I'm pretty good at answering questions."

After a moment's hesitation one of the girls blurted out, "Grandpa said you draw pictures. What kind of pictures do you draw?"

" 'Most any kind," Eric answered. "I guess I'm best at drawing people."

The little girl's face brightened. "Could you draw my picture?"

"If you can find some paper and a felt-tipped pen, I could try."

The children scattered, giggling as they hurried off in search of the materials. "You don't have to do this, you know," Connie said to Eric.

"But I want to. I enjoy entertaining kids." He pulled

out a chair while Connie cleared away a space at the kitchen table. By the time the children returned with paper and pen, he was ready to go to work.

The girl who had asked for a picture was Marie, Milly D'Angelo's youngest child. Eric took a few seconds to study her features before he began to sketch. He worked quickly, using only a few bold strokes. In only minutes he tore the page from the drawing pad and handed it to her.

Marie's face lit up in delight at the sight of the picture. "Look, Mommy. It's me!" she cried out as she ran to show Milly the picture.

Milly turned to Eric in surprise. "I had no idea it would be anything like this."

Connie saw that, while the picture was not a photographic likeness, Eric had captured with a few lines of his pen the essence of the child's appearance. Looking at the picture, she realized that she was seeing a very good piece of work.

When the other children clamored to have their pictures drawn, Eric obliged with a quick sketch of each of them, including a study of Janice's sleeping baby. When the sketches were spread out on the kitchen table, the children's pleasure in seeing their likenesses was only exceeded by that of their mothers.

Janice exclaimed with delight at the pictures of her children; Milly stated proudly that she was going to frame hers. Stella waited until Eric had gone to join the men, and then leaned forward to study the sketches of her grandchildren. "He can draw, all right," she said to Connie in grudging concession, "but what kind of a living can a man make drawing pictures?"

Connie sighed, understanding that Eric had gained no ground with her mother. Stella had made up her mind that he was an unacceptable match for her daughter, and nothing he might do was going to change her opinion.

There was little hope of any help from Sam. He had already made his feelings clear during the conversation at the dinner table. Nor could she expect any support from her brothers. Disconsolately she joined Eric at the end of the evening. His meeting with her family had been a disaster.

To her surprise, Sam came to the door as Eric was leaving. "There's a good ball game on TV Sunday afternoon," he said. "The boys and I will be watching it. Come to dinner and watch the game with us afterward."

Connie bristled at the blunt request. It was more of a directive than an invitation, and she strongly suspected that by convening a family gathering, her father was throwing down a challenge. Eric, however, agreed to the suggestion at once. He thanked Sam for his hospitality and said that he'd be pleased to join the family again on Sunday.

Puzzled, Connie walked outside with Eric and stood on the front porch with him for a moment. Somehow she was as suspicious of his ready acceptance of her father's invitation as she was of Sam's motives in issuing it. Something was going on—something she didn't quite understand—and she wasn't entirely sure what she thought about it.

"You don't have to do this again," she said to Eric, deciding it was a time for candor. "I know what a pain my family is, and there's no reason for you to put up with them."

"There's a very good reason, Connie. They're your family, and they're important to you. That makes them important to me."

"You don't have to pretend. Tonight was a disaster."

"Of course it was. You didn't expect it to be any different, did you? You're the only daughter and the baby of the family. They're not about to sit back and let some strange guy come in and take over."

"It's not their business, Eric. I'm a grown woman, with a right to do what I choose."

"Not to them. You'll always be their baby sister, and any guy who tries to move in on you is going to have a fight on his hands."

Connie sighed unhappily. "There's no reason why you should have to endure all this. It's bound to be as distasteful for you as it is for me."

"I didn't expect them to like me. I knew I was going to face an uphill battle. But you're important enough to me that I'm willing to do whatever it takes to make the things happen for us that I want." Gathering her into his arms, he pressed his cheek against hers. "That is, if you want them to happen too."

"You know I do," Connie whispered, sliding her arms around his waist and nestling her head against his shoulder. During the long evening, she had realized all the more clearly how very important he was to her.

"As long as you're satisfied with me the way I am, I don't have any problems I can't handle."

"I wouldn't change a thing about you," she murmured softly.

He tilted her chin, and his lips found hers, lingering in a long, tender kiss that left her shaken and breathless. As they stood together with their arms entwined, she rested her head contentedly on his shoulder, finding a wonderful kind of happiness in being close to him.

After he had gone, she lingered to enjoy the beauty of the evening, the sweetness of the lilacs that bloomed at the end of the porch, the lacy pattern of moonlight that filtered through the big oak trees in the front yard. There was a special kind of magic in the lovely spring night, and she knew it was there because of Eric.

By the time she went back inside, her brothers had gathered up their families and were preparing to leave. Neither Vic nor Joe said anything about her guest, but Milly smiled at her discreetly as she herded her children out the door. Janice leaned close to whisper as she passed, "He's a great guy, Connie. Go for it."

Sam led his wife upstairs without comment. His atypical lack of opinion was explained when Connie started to her room. Frankie was waiting for her at the foot of the stairs, and his determined expression told her he had been selected as family spokesman.

As she approached him, he called out summarily, ''I want to talk to you, Connie.''

She leveled a cutting glance at him and brushed past him with a terse response. ''Butt out, Frankie,'' she said.

## Chapter Five

Connie was barely awake on Saturday morning when she received a telephone call. "How did it go last night?" an inquisitive Gena Farrell asked.

"You don't want to know," Connie answered with a groan.

"That bad?"

"Worse."

"If you want to talk about it, I'm free for lunch. But if you'd rather I minded my own business, just say so."

Gena's understanding was a welcome balm this morning, and Connie was grateful for her concern. "At this point, I'm very much in need of a sympathetic ear, and I don't think I'm going to get it around here. In fact, the less time I spend around home today, the better off I'll be. You're on for lunch—the earlier, the better.''

They agreed to meet at a tearoom both enjoyed. Connie dawdled in her room until time to leave the house. Cutting off questions by pleading a lack of time, she managed to escape without a session with her mother.

At lunch Gena listened wide-eyed to a description of the family dinner the night before. ''Pop and my brothers deliberately sandbagged Eric,'' Connie finished unhappily. ''They had their minds made up before he ever got there.''

''Wasn't that pretty much what you expected?''

''I didn't expect them to pick him to pieces.''

''Still, it sounds to me like he handled the evening pretty well. He must have been prepared for it,'' Gena observed. ''I guess, after meeting Frankie, he had a pretty good idea of what to expect.''

''Frankie is a pain,'' Connie pronounced resentfully.

''He's being protective. And, from what Eric said to you before he left, he apparently understands.''

''I just hope he'll still be understanding after tomorrow. Pop has asked him to Sunday dinner, and I've got an awful feeling he's going to get a replay of last night—only worse.''

''I'm betting on Eric to handle it. He's a sharp guy.'' Having expressed her opinion, Gena bit with relish into a hot buttered roll.

Connie toyed with her shrimp salad without appetite.

"It's just so underhanded—and so unfair. If it were up to me, I'd tell Pop thanks but no thanks and spare both Eric and myself a miserable day. But Eric seems to want to go through with it."

"I guess he feels it's something he's going to have to deal with sooner or later if he wants to have anything going with you. Apparently you're worth it to him." Gena sighed longingly. "It must be wonderful having a fantastic guy like him willing to put up a fight for you. The rest of us should be so lucky."

This was an often-discussed topic between the two friends, as well as one of some disagreement. "There are plenty of men who are interested in you," Connie pointed out. "One or another of them is always dropping by to see you. In fact, Dr. Foster said he was considering building a glass enclosure around your desk so that your boyfriends couldn't hang out there interfering with your work."

"They just want an excuse to kill time. The good ones never ask me out."

"I thought you were going out tonight with that nice guy who works in administration."

"I am. And he's certainly a nice enough person— if you're interested in hospital accounting and patient statistics."

"From what everyone says, he's really brilliant, Gena. I hear he's the right-hand man to the hospital administrator."

"I know. The trouble is that I'm looking for a thrilling, exciting Superman, and the guys I meet are all Clark Kents.''

''Then that ought to tell you something. Maybe you're looking for the Superman cloak instead of looking at the man in the business suit.'' Connie shook her head in resignation. The conversation had come to a familiar dead end. Although attractive, chestnut-haired Gena had plenty of interested men to choose from, she couldn't seem to find that special person to fill her life.

In contrast to Connie, who was involved with more family than she could deal with, Gena had no ties except for her father, who lived in a distant city and contacted her infrequently. Living alone as she did, with no one to answer to, she found it hard to understand the demands placed on Connie by the large, close-knit D'Angelo family.

''I can promise you one thing. If I'm ever lucky enough to find a gorgeous, exciting man like Eric Lindstrom, nothing's going to come between us,'' she said in an unequivocal tone. Leaning across the table, she added a warning. ''Don't give in to your family, Connie. Don't let them ruin what you have with Eric.''

Dinner at the D'Angelo house started off little better at noon on Sunday than it had on Friday night. Sam herded the family into their same, assigned places and presided once again over the conversation.

''The flowers are nice,'' he commented, pointing to the colorful bouquet that Eric had brought and Connie had arranged as a centerpiece for the dining table. "Stella likes flowers."

"Some I do. Some make me sneeze," Stella said morosely.

Eric only smiled. "Let's hope these don't."

"They probably will," Connie said in irritation. "Mama has a knack for turning joy into despair."

Stella exclaimed indignantly. Sam cast a disapproving glance at his daughter. Turning to Eric, he said, "The pictures you drew of the children are nice too. Their mothers got all excited about them—spent all day yesterday looking for frames."

"The man at the frame shop was very curious about the pictures," Janice spoke up. "When he saw there wasn't any artist's signature on them, he asked who had done them. I'm sorry to say I couldn't remember your last name, Eric."

"Lindstrom," Connie supplied, a bit annoyed at her sister-in-law's lack of tact.

Janice didn't seem to notice. "I'll be sure to tell the man when I go back to get the pictures. He seemed really interested in them. Maybe he wanted to show your work in his shop, Eric. I'll give you his name if you like."

Joe looked at Eric speculatively. "Do you mean there's a market for that kind of a thing?"

"You can never predict what people will buy. I guess it all comes down to a matter of taste."

Sam's interest was captured. "These pictures you draw—is that the kind of thing you teach?"

"The courses I teach are very general, but we spend a little time on illustrations and cartooning."

"I wouldn't think there'd be much demand for that kind of work. How many comic strips do you suppose there's a need for?"

"Not too many. But for those people who are determined to try, there's a small demand for cartoons in newspapers and magazines."

Sam shook his head in disapproval. "If you mean the political cartoons, we can get along without most of them. Especially those like the one that's in the Sunday paper. You know the one that sets me off, Frankie." He turned to his youngest son with a derisive snort. "The one about the little bald-headed guy who wears glasses and has got such a smart mouth."

Frankie grinned. "We know, Pop. That's Lindy. Actually, I think he's pretty good. The guy who draws him knows where the younger people are coming from at least."

"He's full of crazy ideas. That's what he is. And the young people are coming up with enough weird ideas of their own without getting more of them from the funny papers." Sam leveled a reproving glance at Eric. "I hope that's not what you're teaching kids to draw. We don't need any more Lindys in the newspapers."

"I just show them how to lay out a cartoon. I don't

tell them what to draw,'' Eric answered with a good-natured shrug.

Sam turned back to his dinner, and the conversation moved on to talk of the happenings in the family during the previous week. By the time Connie served the dessert of lemon pie, he was in a mellow mood.

Having finished his dinner, he leaned back in his chair. ''The ball game's coming on,'' he announced. ''I thought maybe after we'd watched for a while and your lunch had settled, you boys might want to go out and shoot some baskets.'' He cast a joking glance at his oldest son, Joe. ''Looks like some of you could use the exercise.''

Joe grinned and patted his stomach. ''I guess I need to work off some of Milly's good cooking.''

Vic nodded. ''I could use a good workout myself. Maybe we could get in a game of one-on-one.''

''That okay with you, Eric?'' Frankie asked.

Connie remained silent, but her temper boiled. She knew exactly what her sneaky brothers were up to. They had played basketball since they were children, and all of them were excellent shots. They were going to gang up on Eric and make him look as bad as they could. And with his injured knee, it wouldn't be difficult for them to do it. Not to mention the fact that he had no business playing basketball at all with a weak knee.

Eric, however, agreed with a benign smile. He had no idea he was being ambushed. Connie decided that in decency she had to derail her brother's plans. As soon as she had finished in the kitchen, she and Eric would leave. She wouldn't sit back and let her brothers carry out their underhanded trick.

Eric didn't offer his help in the kitchen today but instead joined the D'Angelo men in front of the television set in the living room. The older two grandsons tagged along after them while the younger children went outdoors to play. Stella, who was doggedly silent in the face of Connie's obvious annoyance with her, watched the baby while Milly and Janice helped Connie with the dishes.

As soon as the kitchen was tidy, Connie began making her excuses to leave. She was ready to go in search of Eric when she heard, coming from the backyard, the sound of male voices and the bouncing of a basketball. She was too late to rescue him. The basketball contest had begun.

"I don't think I want to watch this," she mumbled under her breath, furious.

Janice looked at her questioningly. "Doesn't Eric like to play basketball?"

"It isn't that. I think he said he played some in school, but—" She was ready to explain about the injured knee when, with sudden intuition, she knew that Eric wouldn't want her making excuses for him. She hadn't grown up with three older brothers without learning something about male egos. Whatever the outcome of the basketball game, she knew Eric would want to deal with it on his own.

Refusing to watch, however, she joined her sisters-in-law at the kitchen table. As she listened to the female chatter, she tried not to think what was happening in the backyard at the basketball hoop.

It was hard to concentrate on the conversation when, as time passed, the sound of the male voices in the backyard grew louder. Now and then there was a cheer. Soon the cheers became more frequent, the voices louder and interspersed with bursts of laughter. Gloomily Connie listened as best she could to the talk of babies, recipes, and home decorating. She refused to consider what might be happening to poor Eric.

The talk was interrupted when one of the grandsons ran through the back door into the kitchen. "Wow! You ought to see what's going on out there!" he exclaimed.

Connie jumped up from her chair. "What's happening?"

"About the fanciest kind of shooting I ever saw." Ten-year-old Ricky's eyes were round with excitement. "This guy Eric is something else. Why didn't you tell us he's a basketball coach, Aunt Connie?"

Connie sank back into her chair. "Because I didn't know it," she muttered. "He said something about playing basketball in college, but he didn't say anything about coaching."

"He helps coach the team at Rutherford, and they're

the highest scoring team in town. Now I know why.''
Ricky grabbed a handful of cookies from the pantry
and ran toward the back door. ''I've got to go back
outside so I won't miss anything. Thanks for the cookies, Aunt Connie!''

''Now what do you suppose that was all about?''
Milly asked. She went to the back door and watched
her son hurry toward the cluster of men beneath the
basketball hoop.

Connie and Janice crowded beside her, craning to
see what was going on. It was at once apparent that a
highly spirited contest was taking place. To Connie's
relief, it appeared to be entirely amicable. When one
or another of the men would dribble his way past his
defender to sink a shot, a lusty cheer would go up from
the other contestants. Once, after Eric got off a long,
one-handed shot that whistled cleanly through the bas-
ket, Frankie dropped a congratulatory arm around his
shoulders and shouted, ''Way to go!''

Connie shook her head in disbelief. Four grown men
who minutes before were taking conversational pot-
shots at one another were now frolicking in a classic
display of male bonding beneath a basketball hoop like
ten-year-olds. Seated in a lawn chair, watching them
with a contented smile, was an admiring Sam.

Connie turned away from the door and went back
to the kitchen table. *Men!* she thought disgustedly as,
pouring herself a cup of coffee, she settled in to wait.

She had a feeling it was going to be a while before the game was over.

Stella, who had joined the curious women at the back door, stood for a long time watching the game. The last to return to her seat at the kitchen table, she settled into her chair with a resigned sigh. "Well, at least he knows how to play basketball," she said to Connie with a faint, grudging smile.

It was almost sundown before the jubilant basketball players returned from their play. Following their game, they had sat in the backyard for a lengthy period exchanging stories. By the time they straggled toward the house, a Sunday-evening supper was waiting on the kitchen table. Milly and Janice had set out platters of cheese and cold cuts for sandwiches. Connie had iced down a bucketful of canned sodas and sliced a chocolate cake. The children had been fed and sent out for a last few moments of play before it was time for their families to start home.

Sam watched with satisfaction as the hungry players helped themselves to sandwiches and cake. He was never happier than when surrounded by his family.

Connie noticed at once that there was a new compatibility between her brothers and Eric. They carried on a lively conversation, seeming to have found a number of interests in common. Eric seemed quite at home with her competitive brothers; they seemed to have offered him their wholehearted respect. Even Frankie's former disapproval had been replaced with an open friendliness.

For the first time Connie noticed how tall Eric was in comparison with her brothers. All of the D'Angelo men were over six feet in height, yet he topped them by a least a couple of inches. Remembering how gracefully he had moved during the basketball contest, she realized that the "little bit of basketball" he had referred to must have been quite a lot indeed. Apparently the knee injury he had spoken about had ended a promising sports career.

It was also clear, from the bits of conversation she overheard, that his work with the basketball team at Rutherford School involved much more than a bit of extracurricular time. Eric Lindstrom, she decided, carried his modesty a shade too far. The least he could have done was give her a few hints about himself.

The same thought must have occurred to her father. Sometime while the family was occupied with their supper, Sam sidled over to his daughter. "That fellow of yours is full of surprises. Seems like a person has to learn everything about him the hard way."

"Eric is a very interesting person. He just doesn't talk about himself a lot."

"I wonder how many other things he can do that he hasn't told us about," Sam said, watching Eric speculatively.

"I guess we could always ask him. But then, you've

probably already thought of that,'' Connie suggested with an ironic glance at him.

''It had occurred to me,'' Sam replied with a sly smile.

Connie decided it was time to put in her own claim on Eric's time. She slid her way past her brothers to stand beside him. ''Do you have a little time for me?'' she asked. ''I was beginning to wonder whether you'd forgotten about me.''

''No way,'' he answered, smiling down at her. ''You're the main event. You're what all this is leading up to.''

''Then why don't we ditch this bunch and head for the front porch?''

While she got a serving of cake and a cold drink for each of them, Eric took the opportunity for a word with Sam. As he walked across the room to join her father, Connie noticed that he was limping slightly. Undoubtedly the afternoon's activity hadn't done much to help his troublesome knee. Most likely it was swelling by now. She was ready to suggest an ice pack when once again intuition intervened. Instinctively she knew that he would prefer that she made no mention of it to her brothers.

She waited until they were seated on the front porch, watching the sunset while they enjoyed their cake. Only after she had set aside their plates and they were finishing their sodas did she ask, ''How's the knee?''

He grinned. ''You noticed.''

"How could I miss it? I wondered if it was going to survive the afternoon."

"Only barely. It was very astute of you not to mention it."

"I thought you'd mention it yourself if you wanted anything said about it. Otherwise, short of your collapse, I didn't see any point in bringing it up."

He reached out to take her hand. They sat contentedly, watching the flame-colored sky fade to purple. "You're a very perceptive woman," he said. "Have I told you lately how important you are to me?"

There was a special feeling of assurance in the warmth of his touch. "You're important to me too," she said softly.

They sat for a long time, not talking, simply enjoying the beauty of the spring evening and the contentment of being together. Feeling the strength of his broad shoulder next to hers, the comforting warmth of his touch, Connie knew she had found something rare and special. She forgot about the contention with her parents, the contest with her brothers, about everything except the pleasure of being with him.

She didn't think about his sore knee again until he started to leave. But when he rose from the porch swing, she noticed that he moved painfully toward the front steps. "Oh, Eric. I'm so sorry. I should have done something about your knee. You must wonder what kind of a physical therapist I am to let you sit out here all this time while it's getting stiff and sore."

"Sitting beside you in the porch swing is the best therapy I could have had."

"Still, I could at least take a look at it before you go home."

He shook his head and said wryly, "Better I head for home and the Jacuzzi while I still can. If I work at it, maybe by morning I'll be able to walk well enough to get to my class."

Draping an arm around Connie's shoulders, he limped down the porch steps. She walked with him to his car, lecturing him as he hobbled along beside her. "Anybody with a knee that bad has got to have rocks in his head to go out and play basketball for four straight hours," she grumbled.

"I know. I did it for you."

"I didn't have anything to do with it. You did it so you could show off for Pop and my brothers."

"Of course I did. I had to convince them that I'm not a wimp. Otherwise, I wouldn't have ended up sitting on your dad's front porch holding hands with you."

Connie grinned. "Was it worth the pain and suffering?"

"Every last ache of it. A small price to pay to be with the woman I love." He looked down at her, suddenly serious. "And I do love you, Connie. Very much."

In the moonlight his face was appealing, his smile endearing. In that instant, Connie admitted that this was the man she had waited for, the man she had dreamed of, the man she had fallen irrevocably in love with. "If you want to change your mind, now's the time to do it," she said tremulously, clinging to a last reservation.

His arms only tightened around her. "Not a chance. I know what I want, and I've found it."

"Then I guess that makes two of us," she whispered as she raised her face to his and offered her lips to him.

His lips claimed hers in a long, possessive kiss. As they stood together, arms entwined, hearts beating in unison, Connie felt a wonderful sense of belonging. There surely would be problems ahead of them, but together they could deal with them. As long as they wanted to be together, nothing could keep them apart.

## Chapter Six

Caught up in her newly discovered feelings, Connie floated through the next week on a pink cloud of happiness. "You need a caretaker," Gena Farrell said as she watched her friend move dreamily through her appointments in the PT department. "You put your report on Mrs. Greenway in Mr. Noble's patient folder, and you didn't make any notation at all in Becky Newman's file. Face it, Connie. You're in bad shape."

"I guess I am at that," Connie conceded. "This business with Eric is a new thing for me. I can't seem to get my mind on anything else."

Gena looked at her questioningly. "I take it everything went pretty well for you and Eric last Sunday."

"Well enough. We've still got a way to go with my parents, but the rest of the family seems to be coming around all right. What's important is that Eric and I can hang out at the house now—at least some of the time. It gets expensive to have to go out somewhere every time we want to be together.''

''Do you think money is a problem for him?''

''It doesn't seem to be, although he likely wouldn't say so if it were. Everybody knows, though, that schoolteachers don't make all that much, and I want to carry my part of the expense.''

Gena grinned. ''It's got to be true love. When a woman starts trying to save a man money, things are getting serious.''

Connie brushed aside her friend's teasing, but she returned to her work resolved to share the responsibilities of her relationship with Eric. He shouldn't feel that he had to be constantly taking her to exciting new places. She would be just as content to enjoy his company at home. He needed to know that it was enough for her, simply being with him, and when she saw him tonight after work, she intended to tell him so.

This would be the first time this week that they had been out together. Although Eric had telephoned her several times, there had been no chance for them to see each other. He was occupied with special activities at school; she had been particularly busy at work with extra staff meetings and clinics. Tonight would be all the more special, and she planned to make the most of it.

With an effort she put thoughts of her romance out

of her mind and gave her determined attention to her work. Gena's teasing had jogged her sense of responsibility to her patients. With a heavy schedule of appointments, she spent a long, busy afternoon.

By the time she finished with the last of her patients and hurried to meet Eric, he was waiting for her in the drive-through at the back entrance to the hospital. "I thought, if you had no objection, we might try a new restaurant tonight," he suggested as he headed his van into the evening traffic. "The owner is a friend of mine who has only recently opened the business, and I thought we might help her out. I'm sure the food will be good."

The restaurant turned out to be a modest but inviting place. It was finished in light wood paneling accented with brass lighting fixtures and wall sconces. Lace café curtains drawn on brass rings screened multipaned bay windows. Light wood tables, covered with linen cloths in a soft shade of rose, were centered with rose-colored flowers in green-glass bud vases. Table settings of white china with borders of rose and dark-green were flanked by dark-green napkins and matching green water goblets, providing a pleasing setting for an appealing menu of home-style dishes.

The owner was a young woman whom Eric introduced as Marcia Cooper. She greeted them enthusiastically and seated them at a table in an alcove that overlooked the rest of the dining room. A pleasant waitress served them tall glasses of iced tea and a plate of vegetable appetizers to nibble on while she hurried off to turn in their orders for dinner.

"This is a very attractive place," Connie said to Eric in approval.

He nodded. "Marcia has put a lot of work and thought into it—not to mention some very precious cash. Her husband died several months ago, leaving her with two little boys to raise. She used a good part of the insurance money to start this restaurant, and it's an important venture for her."

"It certainly is a heavy responsibility. I admire her courage," Connie said.

"She's a courageous lady. Her husband, Jack, was a good friend of mine—a really nice guy who ran into a mean disease that he couldn't lick. It was rotten luck for them, but Marcia's trying to put the pieces together as best she can and make a life for her boys."

"Then let's come here as often as we can, and I'll pass the word at work. People at the hospital are always looking for a good place to eat."

"Marcia would appreciate it, I'm sure."

Once again Connie was impressed by Eric's concern for people. He seemed always ready to lend a hand to someone who needed help. "How do you know so many people here in the city?" she asked him with sudden curiosity. "I understood that you hadn't lived here very long."

"I've been here for two years—since I came to teach

at Rutherford. My work brings me in contact with a lot of people.''

It occurred to her then that he talked very little about himself. ''Your work seems to cover a lot of subjects. You teach history, you teach art, and you coach basketball. If I may say so, that's a rather unusual combination of subjects.''

''Not as much as it seems. I only help out with the basketball team. While the school has a good athletic program for the boys, academic subjects come first in hiring faculty, and there's always a need for more help with the sports program. The basketball coach needed an assistant, and I had the time to do something I really enjoy.''

''But what about the history? How are you able to teach art and history both?''

''Again it's a matter of working where I'm needed. There's only a limited demand for art courses at the school, and I'm qualified to teach both subjects. So they were able to fill two spots with one teacher.'' He smiled. ''You could say they killed two birds with one stone except that I don't much like the suggestion. I hope I'm a better teacher than that.''

''I'm sure you are. Rutherford has a reputation for being very selective in their teachers. As a matter of fact, you're rather young to be on their faculty, aren't you?''

He laughed. ''I don't claim any seniority for sure.''

Connie's curiosity was now thoroughly aroused.

"But how did you get on the faculty at all? I wouldn't have thought you'd even know about Rutherford, coming from Florida."

"I'm not from Florida. My parents moved there when my dad retired. Actually, I'm sort of a rolling stone. Our family moved around a lot because of my father's work—in fact, we spent a good bit of time out of the country. I suppose that's where I got interested in history."

"How about the art?"

"It started out as a hobby. I liked to draw pictures when I was a kid, and gradually the interest grew. When it came down to choosing what I most wanted to do, I decided that teaching would best allow me to pursue a career in art. It's risky, of course, but I was willing to take the chance. So far I'm managing to hang in with it."

"I'd say you're doing very well, and I admire you for going after what you really wanted to do. So often people settle for whatever work is easiest to get." Or that paid better, Connie was ready to add, but their conversation was interrupted when their waitress brought their dinner.

The food was as delicious as it had sounded on the menu, and for a time they turned their attention to their enjoyment of the smothered steak and tender vegetables they had ordered. They were waiting to be served their dessert of strawberry shortcake when a question suddenly occurred to Connie.

"If you went to school overseas, how did you manage to play basketball in college?"

"We came back to the States when I started high school. I began playing basketball then and went on with it in college until I hurt my knee. The injury ended my athletic career—such as it was. I still enjoy sports, though, and welcomed the chance to help out with the boys."

"So you ended up as an art-history-basketball teacher."

He hesitated. "Actually, I'm into some other interests too."

Connie laughed. "I've noticed. There doesn't seem to be any end to your interests. Don't tell me you've got still another career."

He didn't answer, seeming suddenly to withdraw from the question. When the waitress arrived with their dessert, he seemed somehow relieved and didn't return to the subject. Connie didn't pursue it, either, having been reminded of a somewhat delicate matter of her own that she wanted to talk about.

She waited until they had sampled their strawberry shortcake to bring up the subject, not knowing quite how to broach it. "There's something I've been wanting to talk to you about. I don't know quite how to put it." She paused to guide a strawberry onto a piece of cake.

He watched her, suddenly attentive. "Just say whatever it is you want to tell me."

She searched for tactful words and, finding none, plunged ahead. "It's just that you've taken me to a lot of wonderful places, Eric, and I've loved every minute of it. But I know it's expensive—going out as often as we do—and I want you to know that I don't expect you to be entertaining me all the time. We can hang out at my house some of the time. I know my family can be a pain, but I can keep them out of our hair."

"I don't have a problem with your family. Getting acquainted with them is just something that's going to take some time."

"I know, and I'll try to make it as comfortable for you as possible. But I want to do my part in sharing the expenses."

He shifted uncomfortably. "It really isn't a problem for me, Connie."

"I don't want to embarrass you," she said quickly. "It's just that it isn't necessary for you to be so extravagant with entertainment."

"I don't consider the way we spend our time together to be a question of entertainment. For me, it's a matter of doing things together that we both enjoy. I feel very lucky to have found someone to share things with, and I honestly don't have any trouble handling what expense there is."

"I just thought . . . I mean, most people have to pay attention to what they spend—" Connie broke off, now embarrassed by her candor.

He hesitated, obviously ill at ease. "Actually, my

situation is a little complicated. Maybe it's time I tried to explain.''

As he searched for words, Connie was relieved to see Marcia, their hostess, coming toward them. When she stopped at their table to speak to them, Eric also seemed relieved.

"How was the food?" she asked them. "And for heaven's sake, tell me the truth. I'm depending on my friends to be honest with me so that I know where I need to improve."

"It was delicious," Connie assured her. "And I love the atmosphere."

"I think you've got a success on your hands," Eric agreed.

"I've got an idea for improving the place, but I'm not sure how to go about it." Marcia paused, seeming reluctant to continue. "I don't how to put this, Eric, but I could really use your help."

"Tell me about it. You know I'll do anything I can."

"Well, it's just that the restaurant doesn't really have a theme. I don't want it to end up being a lunch spot, and if it's going to attract a nighttime crowd, it needs something to set it apart. I had an idea for some original art that might be a little different, but it would depend on getting some of the local artists to contribute."

Eric smiled. "That wouldn't be hard to do. Artists are always eager to show their work."

"I wasn't thinking of traditional landscapes and watercolors, though, and this place definitely isn't right for abstracts. What I had in mind was something offbeat like drawings of sports figures and celebrities—maybe local personalities. Do you think it would work?''

He glanced around the room speculatively. ''Stick to black and white and include some caricatures and humorous sketches—that sort of thing.''

''What I really want is the sort of thing you do.'' Her expression was appealing. ''I realize it's asking a lot, but could you possibly let me use one of your originals? If you contribute, other artists will want their work displayed with yours.''

Eric seemed disconcerted by the request, and he said quickly, ''You know I'll be glad to help you out, Marcia. I'll see what I can come up with.''

''Thanks a million.'' Marcia's voice dropped to a confidential tone, and she glanced at the nearby tables as she leaned down to add softly, ''I won't disclose your identity, of course. I know how you feel about protecting your anonymity.''

He brushed aside her remark, seeming suddenly uncomfortable. ''Give me a little time to think about this, and I'll get back to you. Right now Connie and I need to get going if we don't want to be late for our movie.''

''We've got plenty of time,'' Connie began. But Eric had laid down his fork and was pushing his dessert plate away. Marcia, looking distressed, mumbled an apology and hurried off to speak to their waitress.

Connie had barely finished her dessert when the waitress appeared with their dinner check. Eric, seeming anxious to leave, didn't suggest after-dinner coffee but instead rushed Connie from the restaurant. When, on the drive to the theater, she complimented Marcia's plans for a display of art, he quickly changed the subject.

They arrived early at the movie. While they waited for it to begin, Connie puzzled over Eric's odd behavior. She had no doubt that there was something he didn't want her to know, and she had to wonder what it could be.

She wasn't the only one with questions about Eric, she discovered when the family gathered for its usual Friday-night dinner. After dinner the men retreated to watch a sports program; the women, their work done, sat at the kitchen table while they looked after the children.

"Where is Eric tonight? I thought maybe he might be here," Janice remarked as she enjoyed a second cup of coffee.

"He had to be at school for some sort of program for parents."

"Will he be teaching during the summer?"

"He hasn't said," Connie answered vaguely.

"You two don't seem to find much time for talking," Janice teased.

"We just don't talk a lot about our work," Connie said defensively. "There's not that much to say, really.

He teaches, and I work with patients. There are other, more interesting things to talk about.''

"Besides, what woman wants to spend time talking about work when she's out with a guy who's as good-looking as Eric?'' Janice said with a suggestive grin.

Stella, who had listened to the conversation without comment, looked up from her place at the end of the table to cast a meaningful glance at Connie. ''Good looks make a good cover for things a person doesn't want people to know.''

Milly tried to change the subject. ''Did you ever find out any more about Eric's artwork? From what the man at the frame shop said, he seems to be a really talented artist.''

"Whatever he is, there's a lot he isn't telling,'' Stella muttered darkly.

For once Connie had to agree with her mother. While she had no reason to think he was hiding unpleasant secrets, she had to admit that Eric had told her very little about his personal life. After their conversation with Marcia, she had to believe that he had achieved some success as an artist, but it was obvious that he didn't want her to know about it. Although she didn't question his sincerity in his relationship with her, she did have to wonder why he was so reluctant to talk about himself.

She passed off her mother's remark by changing the subject. To her relief, no more questions were asked about Eric. Still, while she had no reason to doubt him, she couldn't help but be puzzled by the fact that he so mysteriously kept part of his life a secret.

While Connie's unanswered questions about Eric continued to bother her, the subject was not one she found easy to discuss with him. Unwilling to spoil their time together during a weekend that turned out to be particularly enjoyable, she never found the proper moment to bring up her concern.

Nor was there an early opportunity during the following week. Eric spent several nights working, and Connie, tired from a particularly crowded schedule at the hospital, used the time to catch up on her duties at home. It was late in the week before they were able to be together.

Eric arranged to meet her after work in the lounge at the PT department. While she waited for him, she stepped into Dr. Foster's office to report to him on a diagnostic clinic at which she had served that afternoon. They had just finished their conversation and she was leaving the director's office when she saw Eric coming down the hallway. Her eagerness to meet him must have been instantly apparent because Dr. Foster sent her on her way with a friendly directive to enjoy a well-deserved night out.

She thought nothing about the incident until the following morning when Dr. Foster summoned her to his office to discuss one of her patient assignments. They had finished their business and she was turning to leave when he called to her in afterthought, ''By the way, I noticed you leaving the hospital last night with Eric Lindstrom. I didn't know that you were acquainted with him.''

''He's my boyfriend,'' Connie answered, surprised by Dr. Foster's comment. It wasn't like him to concern himself with the staff members' private lives.

His interest was explained when he said, ''I hope you'll tell him how grateful the hospital administrator is for his contribution to the children's wing. His work there has meant a great deal to the kids.''

Not wanting to admit that she had no idea what Dr. Foster was talking about, Connie agreed to pass the message along to Eric and left the office as quickly as she could. But she went back to her work deeply puzzled. This was the first she had heard about any involvement of Eric's with the hospital, and she could only wonder why he hadn't told her about it.

But then there seemed to be a number of things he hadn't told her. In fact, she was only beginning to discover just how many things she didn't know about Eric Lindstrom.

## Chapter Seven

"I don't understand," Connie said to Gena Farrell during a coffee break in the staff lounge. "Why wouldn't Eric tell me he was involved in some project in the children's wing at the hospital?"

Still puzzled by Dr. Foster's remark, Connie had confided her concern to her friend. As always Gena listened with a sympathetic ear. "Maybe he thought you already knew about it," she suggested. "Or maybe he just never thought to mention it."

Connie recalled that Eric had vaguely mentioned having business at the hospital a time or two, but he had never said what it was. Certainly he had said nothing about any business of enough importance to attract Dr. Foster's interest. "I guess what bothers me is *why* he wouldn't want to tell me if he was involved with the hospital in some way," she said. "Why wouldn't he want to share it with me?"

"I'll agree that it's a little strange. But then you have to admit that Eric isn't exactly your everyday, predictable kind of guy. He seems to be into a lot of things."

"Including some he doesn't want to talk about—at least, not to me." Connie turned a troubled face to her friend. "This isn't the first time something like this has come up. There are other things Eric hasn't thought to mention to me."

Gena regarded her thoughtfully. "This really bothers you, doesn't it?"

"You bet it does. There are things going on with Eric that he doesn't want me to know. And I'm beginning to wonder why."

"Surely you don't think he's hiding something important. Like maybe another girlfriend."

"It's nothing like that. I feel sure Eric is up-front about our relationship. It's just that little questions keep coming up about his work—things he's involved in, the people he knows, that sort of thing. I'm beginning to think that maybe he isn't the unpretentious schoolteacher I thought him to be."

"You're not getting bad vibes about him, are you? I mean, maybe having doubts about the kind of person he is or questions about the people he hangs out with."

"Of course not," Connie answered quickly. "Quite the opposite. He takes me to nice places and introduces me to nice people, who all seem to think he's a great guy. The more I know about him, the more I like him. I guess that's why it hurts when I find out there are things he's keeping from me. I've been very open with him, and I want him to be the same with me.''

Gena set down her coffee mug and studied her friend seriously. ''You really care about Eric, don't you? I mean, this isn't just a go-out-and-have-fun-together sort of thing with you anymore. It has gotten serious for you.''

''Eric has become very important to me,'' Connie confessed. ''It would hurt a lot if anything came between us.''

''Then I think you have to be open with him about your doubts. Find out what's going on in his life that you don't know about and deal with it.'' Gena hesitated before she added, ''You may be in for some surprises, you know. Eric could never be called a conformist.''

''He takes life on his own terms. That's for sure,'' Connie agreed.

''He'll never fit into a standard mold, but if you love him, you'll just have to go for it and accept him as he is.''

''But how is he? There's so much I don't know about him,'' Connie said in frustration. ''And that's what bothers me. How come everybody else seems to know so much more about Eric than I do?''

Gena looked at her steadily. ''Isn't that a question you ought to be asking Eric?''

Connie returned to her work deep in thought. As always, Gena's realistic viewpoint had helped her see what she needed to do. Tonight she was having dinner with Eric, and she wasn't going to delay any longer in telling him how she felt. She was going to ask him some questions, and before the evening was over, she intended to have some definite answers.

Eric seemed distracted when he met her after work. He suggested a small, cozy restaurant, which Connie instantly approved. It was a quiet place, run by a French family who concocted delicious meals and provided a quiet, intimate setting. It was the ideal setting for the kind of conversation that she planned to have with Eric.

They talked of inconsequential matters during dinner. Connie was ill-at-ease, waiting for the right moment to bring up the subject she was determined to talk about. Eric either sensed her nervousness or had reservations of his own.

"You're quiet tonight," he said after their waiter had removed their dessert plates and served them after-dinner coffee. "Have you had a difficult day?"

"Not difficult. Just confusing. Something came up that I don't quite understand, and I think maybe you can clarify it for me."

He became suddenly guarded. "I'll try."

"I'm glad to hear it, because I'm hoping you can give me an explanation for a remark Dr. Foster made. He said to tell you how much the hospital administrator appreciates your contribution to the children's wing and how much it has meant to the patients. Since this was the first I'd heard of any connection of yours to the hospital, I could only agree to pass the message along to you." Connie watched him steadily as she added, "Maybe you'd be willing to tell me what he was talking about."

Eric hesitated for a moment before he said with a resigned sigh, "I certainly owe you an explanation—not only about the hospital but about other things too. I guess I should have told you long ago."

"Then whatever it is, I think you'd better tell me now."

He nodded. "We need to talk, Connie, but this isn't the place. It will make things a lot clearer to you if I take you to my apartment where you can see for yourself."

Brushing aside her questions, he escorted her from the restaurant and seated her in his van. The drive to his apartment was made in near silence. Acutely curious and a little fearful of what she might learn, Connie could think of nothing to say. Eric was occupied with his own thoughts.

In minutes he turned into the parking garage of a high-rise apartment in an upscale downtown neighborhood. Built on the fringe of the business section, the enclave of trendy townhouses and condominiums overlooked the bustling, brightly lit city.

The entrance to the garage was guarded by iron-grill

security gates, which swung open after Eric entered a coded serial number into a computerized entry box. They entered the building through another security door. An elevator took them to the top floor of the building, where Eric led the way to the end of the hallway.

When they stepped inside his apartment, Connie was totally unprepared for what she saw. The room, though furnished with a minimum number of pieces, was expensively decorated in an airy, uncluttered style. One wall was composed entirely of glass, providing a magnificent view of the city at night. As she gazed out at the spectacular display of twinkling lights, she blurted out, "This is beautiful. But I don't understand—" She broke off. How could she explain that part of her astonishment came from wondering how Eric could afford to live in a place like this?

He responded to her remark with a dry smile. "I'll admit this isn't quite the setup for a homeless bum sleeping on a park bench."

She flushed. "You know that was an entirely mistaken first impression."

"But this still isn't the kind of place where you would expect a struggling schoolteacher to live."

"To be honest, it isn't. I guess I don't know you as well as I thought I did."

"That's why we're here," he said. "You have a right to know all there is to know about me, and the easiest way to tell you is to show you what I do."

He opened the door to an adjoining room and turned on the light, motioning for her to follow him. Connie stopped in the doorway to gaze around her in amazement. The room, walled on two sides by floor-to-ceiling panels of glass, was furnished with easels, a draftsman's desk, and cabinets filled with art supplies and equipment. Stacks of drawings cluttered a table that extended the length of the room, and dozens of pictures covered the walls. There were quick sketches, black-and-white portrait studies, pen-and-ink drawings, caricatures and cartoons—a variety of graphic art that was clearly of professional quality. There could be no doubt that this was the workplace for a busy artist who produced a considerable volume of work.

"Feel free to look around," Eric invited her. "The pictures will explain things to you better than I can."

She glanced around the room in bewilderment. As she studied the display more carefully, she began to experience a feeling of familiarity. "This one's of Lindy," she exclaimed as she leaned closer to examine a blowup of a captioned cartoon. Looking on, she saw that there were several similar reproductions—all of them featuring the little cartoon character that appeared in the local newspaper.

As she turned to Eric with a question in her eyes, he handed her a stack of storyboard layouts. All of them featured roughed-out sketches of Lindy. "Are you telling me you know the person who draws these?" she asked as she examined the pictures.

For an answer, he opened one of the scrapbooks that were piled on the table. Inside was page after page of Lindy cartoons. ''Look at the signature on the cartoons,'' he directed.

Looking closer, she saw a barely readable signature that spelled out the word ''Lind'' and then trailed off in an indistinguishable scribble. Gazing up at him with dawning comprehension, she murmured, ''Does this signature mean what I think it does? Are you trying to tell me that you're the cartoonist who draws Lindy?''

''I'm afraid so,'' he mumbled, looking uncomfortable. ''I really don't talk about it a lot, but I'm the guy who is responsible for the creation of this little fellow.''

''But I don't understand why you didn't tell me. Why would you want to hide your identity from me?'' A wave of resentment swept over her as she understood that all this time she had wondered about Eric, worried about how he was managing as a modestly paid schoolteacher, tried to encourage him to develop his talent, he was a already a well-known, successful cartoonist.

He ran his hand through his hair, ruffling it distractedly. ''I wasn't hiding anything, Connie. I just never found the right time to tell you.''

''You had any number of opportunities,'' she accused him.

''Not really. Think about it. We didn't get off to the best start. First you thought I was a dropout sleeping on a park bench, then your brother thought I was some kind of lowlife who was coming on to his sister. By the time we got things off the ground, you had let me know what your dad thought about my cartoons. And if you'd left any doubt, the reception I got from him and your mother made it pretty clear what they thought of what I do. Somehow I just never found the right time to come out and say, 'By the way, folks, you know that little roundheaded cartoon character that gravels you so much? Well, I'm the guy who draws him.' "

"But you could have told *me*. All the time we've been going out together, you've never said a word. You've let me and my family make fools of ourselves complimenting what we thought were your amateur drawings of the children when all the time you were a professional artist."

"It wasn't like that, Connie. Be fair. Your family threw up a brick wall against me. Surely you wouldn't expect me to pound on it and tell them to be nice to me because I was a successful artist—especially after they let me know what they thought about a man who made a living drawing pictures."

"But I would expect you to tell *me*. All of your friends—even people at the hospital—knew who you were. Everybody except me. I feel like an utter fool."

"I made a mistake," he said unhappily. "I admit it. But to be honest, I'm still trying to get used to the idea myself. This popularity of Lindy's came on sort of fast for me, and I'm still not very comfortable with it. I guess I'm not too sure it's going to last.''

There was an uncertainty in Eric's expression, a vulnerability that tugged at Connie's sympathy in spite of her hurt feelings. She could understand why he might be reticent about his success, and she could understand why he wouldn't be comfortable talking about it to her family.

As she flipped through the scrapbook, looking at the dozens of cartoons, she had to admire not only the talent but also the intellect that had created them. Lindy's familiar little bespectacled figure with his stooped shoulders, rumpled clothing, and meek expression had become a symbol. With his funny looks and dejected expression, he was a spokesman for the average person who was struggling to cope with the insensitivity of a cynical world.

Looking at the popular little cartoon character, she understood that only a keen, perceptive mind could have conceived him. Eric Lindstrom was not only a very talented man, he was a truly unusual one.

But then, hadn't she already discovered that? From the beginning she had known that Eric was a unique individual with an uncommon perception of life. As she looked down at the scrawled, incomplete signature on the cartoons, she could only wonder that she hadn't recognized it at once.

She looked up at Eric, who was watching her expectantly, but she couldn't find the proper words to express her feelings, her admiration, her awe of him. She shook her head in wonder. "How could I have failed to guess? You gave me dozens of clues. I feel so stupid not to have figured it out for myself."

He gestured awkwardly around the room. "Well, now you know. This is what I do. It seemed better to show you than to try to tell you."

Gazing at the display of art, Connie was besieged by questions. Questions about Eric the artist, Eric the teacher, Eric the very talented man. "Lindy is named after you, of course. How long have you been drawing him?"

"From the time I was a kid, I guess. I always liked to sketch likenesses of people—people I knew, people I saw who had interesting faces. By the time I was in my teens, I was going to parks, cafés, and the like doing sketches of the people and things I saw. I would see someone in a crowd and wonder what his life might be like, what problems he might have, what kind of a person he was.

"Gradually Lindy's personality formed in my mind, and he became a cartoon character. I started drawing him when I was in college, and the school paper used my cartoons. The local paper picked it up, then some regional papers, and then a syndicate."

"So that by the time you came here to teach, Lindy was already recognized," Connie said, beginning to understand.

Eric nodded. "The school offered me a chance to

teach graphic art, and I could keep up with my work as a cartoonist. It was a very good deal for me, and I hope I've been able to give something to my students.''

''And the history class?''

''I've been filling in for a semester, since I had enough college credits to be qualified to teach it.''

''Which accounts for some of Lindy's ideas about current affairs.''

''Lindy just comments on society. He doesn't try to tell anybody what to think.''

''Especially people like Pop?'' she asked with a wry glance at him.

He shrugged. ''Lots of people aren't going to agree with Lindy's philosophy. Maybe most of them don't even like him. But that's the way it is with cartoons, and cartoonists just have to get used to it. Maybe this time next year nobody at all will be interested in Lindy.''

''I don't think so,'' Connie said as she looked at the display of artwork on the walls. ''I think Lindy is going to be around for a very long time. And even if he isn't, I think there's very little limit to all the wonderful things you're going to create.'' A little shiver of fear ran through her as she looked at the man who had come to mean so much to her. How could a plain, ordinary woman like herself even hope to hold the interest of someone as handsome, talented, and magnetic as he was?

Quietly she placed the scrapbook on the table and

turned away from the studio with its unsettling revelations. She went back into the living room to stand before the window, looking out at the lights of the city. Looking out into the night, she felt suddenly very lonely and afraid. Of all the men out there among the glittering lights, why had she chosen Eric Lindstrom to fall in love with? How could she hope to hold any lasting attraction for this man whose talent was going to take him to the highest peak of success when she was only one of the many unremarkable people destined to spend unremarkable lives in the valley filled with ordinary people?

Eric came to stand beside her. "I'm sorry I wasn't as open with you as I should have been. If there's anything at all you still don't understand, I'll try to explain. I don't want there to be any more misunderstanding between us."

"I don't think I want to hear any more. I feel like a big enough fool for one night," she said forlornly.

"If anybody is a fool, it's me. It never occurred to me that you might think I was trying to deceive you. It was just that this is something that I find hard to talk about, and I didn't see that you might feel I was being dishonest with you." His arms stole around her, and he rested his cheek against her hair. "But at least it's all out in the open now and we can put it behind us. I'm just glad we've got it straightened out so we can get on with our future."

"But don't you see, Eric? Everything is changed.

You're a very different person from the one I thought you were, and I'm not even sure we have a future.''

His arms tightened around her. ''Oh, but we do. Nothing can change the fact that we belong together. Don't you understand that, without you, there isn't any future for me? None of this means anything to me if I can't share it with you.''

Connie settled into his arms and yielded her lips to his, but even as he claimed them, her heart was heavy. Although Eric might truly believe that nothing stood between them, a barrier now existed. Knowing how very different from each other they were, she had to wonder if there could ever be anything lasting between them.

## Chapter Eight

Connie went to work the next morning heavy-hearted. Although Eric had done his best to convince her that nothing had changed between them, she still felt a dull sense of betrayal. Maybe he was, as he had insisted, the same man as he had been before; he just wasn't the man she had thought him to be.

She could sympathize with his problem in dealing with the uncomfortable situation in which he found himself. From the beginning he had been the victim of misunderstandings. She had, at the outset of their acquaintance, misjudged him; her family's cool reception had at once put him in a defensive role. Once begun, the misconceptions had snowballed.

Yet, while she understood his awkward position, she couldn't help feeling deceived and rejected. Regardless

106

of his problems with her family, he should have confided in her and trusted her to understand. Even if he hadn't deliberately deceived her, it hadn't occurred to him that she might feel foolish and left out.

And she did feel foolish to have so ignorantly misled her family about Eric. She had created a situation that was going to be an embarrassment to all of them. Although the D'Angelos were plainspoken, they were basically polite people. They might not have cared for Eric's cartoons or agreed with the views that were depicted in them, but they would never have belittled his work in his hearing. She hated to think how they were all going to feel when they found out who Eric was, and she dreaded the moment when she was going to have to tell them.

Her work was, as always, an antidote to her troubled feelings, and she was able to put her problems aside for the day. It was only after her workday was over that she let herself think about the unpleasant task that awaited her that evening. It was Friday, and the family would be gathering for dinner. In conscience, she had to explain to them what she had learned about Eric. She had brought him into her home and encouraged them in a totally mistaken impression of him. Now she owed it to them to explain who he was.

Although she hadn't told Eric what she intended to do, he had surely guessed when she asked him not to join the family that evening. Nor had she agreed to any plan to see him on Saturday. She could tell that he was hurt, but it couldn't be helped. She first had to handle her obligation to her family before she could deal with her own feelings.

She arrived home early to prepare dinner, saying little as the family gathered. Her thoughts were occupied with the unpleasant task that lay ahead of her. She could only wonder how she was to find the proper moment for the announcement she had to make.

Her mother solved the problem for her. When it was time to set the table for dinner, she looked sharply at Connie as she noticed the absence of a plate for Eric. "He's not coming again—the artist?"

"Not tonight, Mama."

Stella's expression sharpened. "Two weeks he isn't here. Maybe he doesn't like to be with the family."

"He likes the family just fine. I didn't invite him tonight."

"You didn't want him to come?" Stella's face brightened hopefully.

Connie took a deep breath. Now was as good a time as any to bring up the unpleasant subject. "That isn't the reason, Mama. There are some things I wanted to tell the family about Eric, and I thought it best if he wasn't here."

The clatter of china and silver stilled. Her mother and sisters-in-law looked at her curiously. "Everything's okay, isn't it?" Janice finally asked.

"I guess that depends on your point of view. There's

something more you need to know about Eric. He's not exactly as uncomplicated a person as he seems.''

''I knew it!'' Stella exclaimed. ''He's got a wife already!''

''Of course not,'' Connie said impatiently. ''Eric is everything he said he was. It's just that there's a little more that I haven't told you.''

She paused to grope for words. Janice moved to her side and placed a comforting hand on her shoulder. ''Just tell us what it is, Connie, and we'll understand.''

''You know those pictures Eric drew of the children—the ones the man at the frame shop asked you about?'' Connie began haltingly. ''Well, the man was right about them. It seems that Eric's work is fairly well-known in art circles around town.''

''I thought so,'' Milly spoke up excitedly. ''Joe said those pictures could be worth something.''

''You mean that Eric is a famous artist?'' Janice's interest quickened.

''He's a special kind of artist. Actually. . . .'' Connie girded herself for the explanation.

''He draws pictures of naked women!'' Stella cried out in alarm.

Connie sighed resignedly. ''It's nothing like that, Mama. He's a cartoonist.''

The three faces became puzzled. ''You mean, like in the funny papers?'' Stella asked.

''Like on the editorial pages.'' Now committed, Connie plunged ahead. ''You know the cartoon character we talked about when Eric was here to dinner—the one named Lindy?''

''The one Pop dislikes so much?'' Janice's eyes widened in consternation.

''That's the one.''

Janice gasped. ''You mean. . . .''

Connie nodded gloomily. ''Eric is the person who draws it.''

''Eric draws Lindy?'' Milly exclaimed in disbelief.

''Who's this Lindy?'' Stella demanded.

''It's the cartoon Pop gets so mad about every Sunday when he reads the paper. He claims the guy who draws it is a nut.'' Milly clapped her hand over her mouth and looked at Connie in embarrassment at what she had said.

A silence fell as the women considered the significance of Connie's announcement. Janice broke it at last. ''Vic likes the cartoon. And so does Frankie. I remember he said so at the table that night when Pop told Eric what he thought about it. . . .'' Her voice trailed off lamely.

''And what he thought about the crazy ideas of the cartoonist,'' Connie finished for her. ''Now you get the idea.''

''Let me get this straight,'' Stella spoke up. ''You're saying that your boyfriend, the artist, draws that cartoon that sets Sam off every time he sees it? You're telling me it's his fault that every Sunday of my life

I've got to listen to Sam carry on about the state of the world for half the morning?''

''Eric draws the cartoon, Mama. It's not his fault if it sends Pop into orbit.''

''Of course it is. He shouldn't draw things that aggravate people that way.''

''The cartoon doesn't aggravate everybody the way it does Pop. Some people like to read it.''

''Some people will read anything. That's no reason to put aggravating things in the newspaper,'' Stella said resentfully.

''Well, whether you like it or not, Lindy is in the newspaper, and Eric is the artist who draws it. I just thought you ought to know.'' Hoping to end the discussion, Connie turned to the kitchen and started serving dinner.

When she took her seat at the dining-room table, however, she discovered that the subject was not to be put to rest. As she looked down the length of the long table, she saw that her brothers were eyeing her steadily as her father glowered at her in disapproval. ''Your mother has been telling me things about Eric. Is it true what she says?''

''I guess it depends on what she says,'' Connie answered defensively.

''According to her, Eric is the guy who draws the Lindy cartoons,'' Frankie spoke up. ''How come he didn't tell us?''

''I suppose because he didn't think Pop would be

very happy to hear it, feeling as he does about the cartoons.''

''I see what you mean,'' Frankie said with a grin.

An awkward silence fell over the table. Sam ate his dinner with a stony expression. After a while he looked up from his plate. ''Is that why Eric isn't here tonight?'' he asked Connie.

''I told him not to come. I thought I ought to tell you all who is he.''

''You should have told us before,'' Sam said gruffly. He turned back to his dinner and ate silently, his expression unreadable. Connie could only guess whether he was angry, annoyed, or maybe somehow disappointed.

The meal seemed to go on interminably. Although nothing more was said about Eric, Connie sensed an embarrassment among the family members. It was a relief when the dinner hour was over and she could return to the kitchen.

Her sisters-in-law joined her in tidying the kitchen. The conversation was stilted, none of them seeming to know what to say. Stella sat at the kitchen table, occupying herself with her own thoughts as she quietly drank her coffee.

Janice finally broke the silence. ''I just wish you had told us who Eric is, Connie. I feel like an utter idiot, encouraging him to do something with his art.''

''He appreciated your interest. Actually, he's a little self-conscious about what he does. He doesn't talk much about it.''

"He doesn't talk much about himself, either," Milly remarked. "I wonder what else there is that he hasn't told us. Maybe we're in for some more surprises."

"Let's hope he's fresh out of surprises," Connie said dryly.

"With him, who can say?" Stella spoke up suddenly. "I knew he was hiding something. He's a man who holds himself back. But it's not so bad, Connie. It could have been worse." She rose from her chair with a sigh and, rubbing her back, went to the dining room to play with the children. Connie understood that, as far as her mother was concerned, the subject had been settled.

To Connie's relief, her sisters-in-law took up the conversation and turned it to other matters. Nothing more was said about Eric until the end of the evening when Vic and Janet were herding their little ones to the front door. Before they left, Janice dropped back to speak to Connie. "I'm glad you told us about Eric. I think what he does is really exciting. The only thing I don't understand is why you didn't tell us about it sooner."

"I didn't know about it myself until last night."

A look of understanding came into Janice's eyes. She dropped a comforting hand on Connie's shoulder. "It'll be all right as soon as Sam gets used to the idea. It will all work out. You'll see."

Connie wished she could be as confident of her parents' reaction as her understanding sister-in-law, but she had her doubts. As soon as her brothers and their families had gone, Sam and Stella went upstairs to their room without further discussion. Neither of them had any questions for her; neither of them mentioned Eric. They were keeping their thoughts to themselves.

She found an unexpected ally in her brother Frankie. She had turned out the light in the kitchen and was on her way to her room when he sidled past her in the hallway. "I think it's really cool about Eric. He's a good guy," he said. "Don't worry about Mom and Pop. They'll come around."

Connie was grateful for her brother's support, but she wasn't so sure things were going to be all right. Her parents' odd silence told her that their reactions were still to be dealt with. And even if they accepted Eric, she now had her own doubts.

Nothing would change her feelings for Eric. There could never be another man for her. It was just that she had fallen in love with a man whose hopes and ambitions she had believed in, whose life she could be an important part of. But Eric didn't need her to encourage his talent or work beside him to build a future. He had already managed it all very nicely on his own. There was nothing an ordinary woman like her could give him. She could only be a bystander in his life.

Sunday was long and dreary, clouded by a late-spring rain. It was a day of quiet at the D'Angelo house, since the family didn't usually gather there on Sundays.

Frankie, as was his custom, was spending the day with his friends, and Connie spent a lonely day puttering in her room. Feeling as she did, she had refused to go out with Eric over the weekend. Until she'd had time to sort out her feelings, she didn't want to see him. She couldn't commit any more of herself to him until she knew whether there was going to be a future they could share.

By afternoon she was wandering the house, looking for things to do. She had cleaned her room and caught up on her laundry; there were no meals to be prepared. Television held no interest for her and, with her thoughts as confused as they were, she couldn't concentrate on reading. She didn't even have the heart to look at the Sunday newspaper, unable to face the reminder of Eric that it held within its pages. The day stretched out bleakly, and the hours crawled dismally past as the rain continued. It was almost four o'clock when the tedium was interrupted by a visitor.

Connie, clad in a worn pair of jeans and a baggy T-shirt, answered the door. She stepped back in surprise when she saw Eric standing on the front porch. Her heart gave a lurch at the sight of him. He looked unbelievably handsome in neatly pressed khakis and a knit shirt that exactly matched the blue of his eyes. With his broad shoulders outlined by the trim fit of the shirt and his blond hair dampened by the rain, he held a heart-wrenching appeal.

Acutely aware of her shiny nose and rumpled attire,

Connie raised a hand to smooth her tousled hair and blurted out, "I wasn't expecting you."

"I don't know why. You didn't honestly think I was going to let you do this to us, did you?" Eric asked as he pushed his way past her into the hallway. "You and I have to talk, Connie. There's a lot we have to get straightened out. But first I need to explain things to Sam."

"You don't need to. I told the family about you Friday night."

"Then it's all the more important that I talk to him," Eric insisted.

"I don't think this is a good time," Connie said doubtfully.

"I can't think of a better one," a voice called out from behind her. She turned to see her father standing in the hallway. "Come in, Eric. I was wondering where you were." Although his tightly controlled expression revealed no anger, he didn't smile.

He ushered Eric into the living room and offered him a seat on the sofa. When Connie would have left them to their talk, he indicated the place next to Eric. "Sit down, Connie. You're in on this too." Picking up the remote control to the TV set, he turned off the golf match he was watching and settled into his easy chair, swiveling it around to face the two of them seated uncomfortably side by side.

"There are some things I need to tell you," Eric began.

"There's more? Connie's already told us you're a highfalutin cartoonist," Sam said gruffly. "You should have told us, Eric."

"I came over here that first night ready to tell you about myself, but the conversation swung around to where I couldn't quite find a way to do it without embarrassing all of us."

"I'd rather have had my hand called for putting down your cartoons than to have made a fool of myself," Sam said in a wounded tone. His expression clearly revealed his hurt feelings. "You ought to have told us right off who you were."

Eric met his accusing gaze steadily. "I did tell you who I was. There's not a single thing I've told you that isn't true. I left out one single fact about what I do for a living. That's all."

"A mighty important fact," Sam grumbled, unswayed.

"All I ever asked of you was to be accepted for the person I am, and I'm the same person I've always been. Nothing about me has changed. Maybe you don't think much of what I do for a living, but you weren't too crazy about it before. So I can't really see that anything is different." Eric smiled faintly. "Look at it this way. At least, if you don't like what my cartoons say, you can argue with me about them now."

"I don't take issue with what you say in your cartoons. A man's got a right to his opinions. It's just that you ought to have told me."

Eric sighed. "I may be a lot of things you don't like, but I'm not stupid. I've got better sense than to walk into a grizzly bear's den and tell him to come get me. Admit it, Sam. I was about as welcome as the plague around here, with you and Stella and Connie's brothers all lined up against me."

Sam was silent for a long moment. "I guess you've got a point," he said finally. "Maybe both of us have got some apologizing to do."

"That's why I'm here. I want to set things right with you if I can."

Sam cast a glance at Connie's unhappy face. "It looks to me like there's somebody else you need to set things right with first. You and I can get back to each other later." He waved an arm in a gesture of dismissal. "Go along, you two, and talk this out."

Reluctantly Connie followed Eric outside and sat down beside him on the porch swing. They sat silently for a time, listening to the patter of the rain as it dripped from the eaves. When Eric picked up her hand, she didn't resist him.

"Talk to me, Connie," he said. "I know I put you in an awkward position with your family, but I hope you care enough about me not to let your pride come between us."

"It isn't a matter of pride," she said sadly. "It's just that you're not who I thought you were."

"That doesn't make sense. Nothing about me is different."

She shook her head. "Everything about you is different. You're not just an ordinary teacher; you're a successful, well-known artist."

"Would you rather I was a vagrant sleeping on a park bench?" he asked impatiently.

"Of course not. But I did think I had a lot in common with a schoolteacher."

"And you don't have anything in common with a cartoonist?"

"That's what I'm wondering."

He tilted her chin and forced her to meet his gaze. "Is there something wrong with being a cartoonist?"

She swallowed hard and looked away. "It isn't that there's something wrong with it. I just don't see where I fit into that kind of life-style."

"It isn't a life-style. It's a job. It's simply the way I make my living," he said in frustration. "My life is what you and I have. Our life-style can be whatever we want it to be."

"Can it, Eric?" she asked fearfully.

"Of course it can." He took her hands in his and looked deeply into her eyes. "You know how important you are to me, and I believe I'm important to you. We've got something really special, and I hope we're smart enough not to let it get away from us."

Gazing up at him, Connie couldn't doubt his sincerity. "I don't want it to get away," she whispered.

"Then let's work this out together. Staying apart and brooding isn't going to bring us closer."

"I'm willing to try," she said in concession.

"Then let's begin tonight. Come out with me and start sharing the things I do. I promised to give a sketch to Marcia Cooper for her restaurant, and I'd like you to come with me when I take it to her."

Looking at his intent face, Connie couldn't refuse him. Although she still felt a barrier between them, she knew she didn't really have a choice. She had to make it work with Eric, because without him she wasn't sure how much of a life she could have at all.

*Chapter Nine*

Connie set out for the evening with rising spirits. Her outlook had been improved by a bubble bath, a fresh hairdo, and a new dress in a cheerful shade of daffodil yellow. To add to the occasion, the rain had stopped, leaving the city streets with the fresh-washed scent of spring. The first stars were appearing in a clear navy sky by the time they arrived at Marcia Cooper's restaurant.

Marcia's face brightened as they entered. When she saw the portfolio Eric carried, she broke into a smile. "Is that what I hope it is?" she asked excitedly as she hurried to find them a table.

"It's what you asked for," Eric replied. "I hope you like it."

After he had seated Connie at the table, he opened

the portfolio and took out a large pen-and-ink drawing that bore his scribbled signature in one corner. The familiar round, bespectacled face of his little cartoon character looked out at them. With a napkin tucked under his chin, a knife in one hand and a fork in the other, Lindy was looking down with an intimidated expression at the indignant lobster that was marching off his plate.

"I love it," Marcia exclaimed. "It's exactly what I hoped for."

"I also talked to some of the artists at Victorian Corner. They all liked your idea, and several of them were interested in contributing to your collection. If you'll drop by their studios, you can pick out some things you like." Eric took a card from his pocket and handed it to her. "Here's the information you'll need to get in touch with them."

Marcia's eyes shone. "I can't tell you how much I appreciate this. How can I possibly thank you?"

"Easily. Get your chef to stir up two servings of his special veal dijon and save us two pieces of your caramel icebox pie."

"With pleasure. His as well as mine." Marcia hurried off gratefully to see to the order.

"You've made her a happy woman," Connie said as Eric sat down at the table. "It was a very thoughtful thing for you to do. And I particularly liked your drawing of Lindy."

"So maybe you've decided Lindy's not so bad after all?" he asked with a tentative smile.

"I never said he was. I've always loved him."

"How about the guy who draws him? Are you having any similar feelings for him?"

"Oh, yes," Connie said softly. "He's very lovable too."

"I'm glad to hear it. I was beginning to wonder if there was any hope for him." He reached across the table to cover her hand with his.

At the warmth of his touch, the misunderstanding between them faded. Connie forgot her hurt feelings, her doubts and fears, as she lost herself in the enchantment of being with him.

After dinner they went to a romantic movie where they held hands and Connie cried over the sentimental ending. Afterward they lingered over cups of Viennese coffee at a favorite coffeehouse. It was late when Eric finally parked his van in the driveway at the D'Angelo house and they walked hand in hand to the front door.

Eric drew her into his arms and kissed her tenderly. "I hope we've put our troubles behind us, because I don't want to spend another weekend like this one," he said. "I'll have to tell you that it was bleak without you."

"I didn't enjoy it, either," Connie admitted. "I guess I've gotten pretty hung up on having you around."

"And that's where I intend to be, Connie. I warn

you that I'm not going to let anything come between us.''

She rested her head against his shoulder, loving the feel of his arms around her and the sweetness of his lips against hers. She still wasn't sure they'd solved all their problems, but she was ready to do whatever it took to deal with them.

The next day at work, Connie acted on her resolution by paying a visit to the children's wing at City Medical Center. Now determined to learn everything there was to know about this complex man she had fallen in love with, she was acutely curious about his connection with the hospital. If Dr. Foster had been so impressed by the contribution he had made to the children, she wanted to see for herself what he had done.

She found a few free minutes late in the morning to drop in on the playroom in the children's wing. A hospital volunteer was entertaining a group of the children, who were seated at a table busily working with crayons on long strips of paper. When Connie stopped at the table to inspect the drawings they were making, she saw that the papers were covered with little stick figures. Some of the figures were clearly doctors and nurses; others seemed to be children receiving treatment. Finished pictures were mounted on the walls of the room, depicting the children's experiences at the hospital.

Connie saw then that a group of pencil sketches occupied one section of the wall. Each was the picture of a child's face. Instantly she recognized Eric's bold style in the character studies, his familiar signature scrawled in the corner of each picture.

"I see these were drawn by Eric Lindstrom," she said to the volunteer.

"He's been in several times to do sketches of the children. They love to look at the pictures of themselves, so we put them up in here so they can see them. When a child is released from the hospital, he gets to take his picture with him. It has come to be an exciting moment for the kids when a picture comes down and one of them goes home."

Connie took a moment to admire the sketches and then went back to the table where the children were at work. "They seem to like drawing their own pictures," she remarked.

"Mr. Lindstrom encourages them to draw whatever they can in any way they can. They work hard to have something to show him when he returns," the volunteer explained. "The interesting thing is that most of the pictures they draw are pictures of themselves. The psychologist who works with them says the drawings they make are very helpful in finding out how the children feel about their illnesses and helping them deal with them."

Connie left the children's wing deeply impressed by the work Eric was doing and by his generosity in sharing his time and talent with others. It was no wonder Dr. Foster had been so complimentary about the project. She went back to work feeling a warm sense of pride in the exceptional man she had come to love so much.

Gena Farrell was equally impressed when Connie told her about Eric's contribution to the children's wing.

"It's a wonderful thing for him to do for the kids," she said when Connie had finished her report. "I'm surprised we hadn't heard anything about it, though. He certainly can't be accused of seeking out publicity."

"I'm finding that Eric is very modest about his work. He doesn't say much about what he does."

"Apparently he's finally willing to talk to you about it. That's a step in the right direction." Gena cast an inquiring glance at Connie. "I take it that he's answered some of those questions that were bothering you."

Connie nodded. "We had our ups and downs for a little while, but we're getting it all worked out. At least, I think we are."

"I hope so, because I can see where he found himself in a tight spot." Gena shrugged philosophically. "Don't be too hard on him, Connie. He's a good guy. There are women out there who would lap him up like a cat after a can of sardines. Believe me, I speak from the viewpoint of one of them. The pickings are pretty slim from where I sit."

Connie had to smile. "You have more men to pick

from than any woman I know, Gena. When was the last time you stayed home on a Saturday night?''

''But when did I have an honest-and-true romantic evening with a guy who made my heart beat faster and made me run out to buy a new dress?'' Gena shook her head. ''Be honest, Connie. Finding someone you really care about is hard to do. There aren't too many men like Eric around.''

Thinking of being with Eric in the moonlight the night before, Connie had to agree. ''I won't argue with you about that. I won't deny that he's special.''

''Then don't forget it,'' Gena warned. ''Some women never have a chance for the kind of happiness you've found.''

''I just want to be sure that things can work out for us.''

''Then be willing to give a little to make them work. I promise you that if I'm ever lucky enough to find what you've got with Eric, I won't let anything—or anybody—stand in the way.''

While Gena had always been tactful in her remarks, she had never made a secret of her opinion that Connie's family imposed upon her. But independent Gena with no ties and no family of her own had little appreciation of the warmth and support to be found in a close-knit family. It wasn't as if Sam and Stella were being deliberately arbitrary in accepting Eric. They simply wanted her to be safe and secure in her relationship with him. It would be up to her and Eric to help things along. They would have to prove to her parents that he was the right man for her and that they belonged together.

With the ending of the school year, Eric had more time to spend with Connie. Now determined to bring her fully into his life, he had a long list of places he wanted her to visit and dozens of people he wanted her to meet. They became regular visitors to quaint Victorian Corner, and Connie became acquainted with his many friends there. She found the artists involved in the project to be a fascinating group of people and soon was comfortably joining in their talk about their various interests.

Eric was equally dedicated to proving himself with Connie's family. He joined in family gatherings and soon formed an easy friendship with her brothers. He continued to be a favorite with Janice and Milly, and the D'Angelo children, of course, adored him.

Sam's reservations also seemed to disappear, and he accepted Eric into his family. Although he never made a comment about Eric's Lindy cartoons, Connie noticed him peeking surreptitiously at them when he read his Sunday paper.

Stella was the only member of the family who refused to be won over. While she was never openly discourteous to Eric, there still was a grudging reserve in her manner. And even though she never criticized him in Connie's hearing, there were times when she could be heard muttering indistinguishable comments about him under her breath.

Otherwise, events were proceeding as Connie had hoped. The D'Angelos were for the most part accepting Eric into their circle wholeheartedly, and she was winning a place for herself among his friends.

It was at the beginning of June on a moonlit Saturday night that Eric began the evening with a surprise. "What would be your chances of getting a week off from work?" he asked. "I'd like you to go to Florida with me and meet my parents."

"I'm due some vacation time and can certainly ask Dr. Foster for some time off. When did you want to go?"

"As soon as possible. Do you think you can swing it?"

"I can try. I must say, though, that you've taken me by surprise. You haven't said anything about wanting to go anywhere—much less about wanting me to go with you."

"I'm sorry not to be able to give you more notice. I had to wait until I was sure I had everything worked out. You know that I've been wanting you to meet my parents—and, of course, they're eager to meet you. My mother will be writing you right away with an invitation to visit them."

Connie felt a moment's uncertainty. Suppose Eric's parents didn't like her? Reminded of Stella's cool reaction to Eric, she for the first time fully sympathized with his unfortunate introduction to her family. She wondered uneasily how she would react if faced with the same rejection.

When she tentatively mentioned her concern to Eric, he brushed it aside lightly. "My parents are delighted I've found the right woman at last. They'll love you as much as I do."

"But what if they don't?"

"It wouldn't matter. My parents are much more detached from me than yours are from you. I'm not suggesting that we aren't close and that we don't care very deeply for one another. It's just that they have a busy life of their own apart from me and are perfectly content for me to lead the life I choose."

"I can't imagine having that kind of relationship with your parents. It must be nice to be free to live however you like and still have their blessing," Connie said enviously.

"It's easier for sons. You're the youngest, and you're the only daughter. Your parents are finding it hard to realize that their youngest child has grown up and is ready to leave the nest." He reached out to cover her hand with his as he added, "And you'll be leaving very soon if I have anything to say about it."

"Will I, Eric?" Connie asked dreamily.

He grinned. "What do you think this trip to Florida is all about?"

"I thought it was to be a vacation," she teased.

"That too. But it's time for us to be making plans for our future. Definite and permanent plans."

Agreeing wholeheartedly, Connie excitedly set about implementing those plans. On Monday morning she arranged with Dr. Foster to take time off from work the following week. Eric made airline reservations, and their vacation was set in motion. They would take a Friday-evening flight to Florida for their visit with his parents and a week of relaxation at the beach.

The next few days were spent in a rush of activity as Connie shopped for beach clothes and a new bathing suit. Eric suggested that she take along a couple of dresses for the entertainments his mother planned. Her excited anticipation of the vacation heightened until midweek when the promised note of invitation from Mrs. Lindstrom arrived.

Up until then, Stella had observed her daughter's preparations without comment. While she displayed an obvious lack of enthusiasm concerning the vacation plans, she expressed no disapproval. With the arrival of the note, however, her silence ended.

She was waiting in the kitchen, note in hand, when Connie arrived home from work. "This came for you today. It's from those people in Florida," she said. She waited impatiently while Connie read the note.

"It's from Eric's mother, inviting me to stay with them. She said she was going to write." Having satisfied her mother's curiosity, Connie started from the room.

Stella intercepted her. "How can you be thinking of going off to stay with strangers?" she demanded as she jabbed at the note with a forefinger. "You don't even know these people."

"That's why Eric is taking me to Florida, Mama. He wants me to meet them."

"Why does it take a week to meet them? A day would be enough."

"Eric wants us to have time to get really acquainted. And they have things planned for us to do and people for us to see. They don't have Eric with them all that much, you know."

"All the more reason for you not to be there. His parents need some time alone with their son."

"I'll see that they get plenty of time with him. Besides, this is the way Eric wants it. It's important to him for us all to be together."

"You'll be sick of each other long before the week is out," Stella predicted sourly.

"I don't think so," Connie said with a resigned sigh. "I've talked to the Lindstroms on the telephone, and they seem to be very pleasant people."

"Pleasant is as pleasant does. You'll see."

Having spoken her piece, Stella left the kitchen and went to her bedroom. She spent the rest of the evening lying down, leaving it to Connie to set out her father's dinner before she went out for the evening with Eric. For the remainder of the week Stella spent most of her time in her room, saying little to the family. When

Connie and Eric departed on Friday evening, she didn't come downstairs to bid them good-bye.

"Your mother isn't feeling well. Her back is bothering her," Sam explained. "She said to tell you to have a nice trip."

Connie felt certain her mother was simply sulking, but she had no doubt of her father's sincerity when he hugged her warmly, shook hands with Eric, and wished them a pleasant vacation. Putting her concerns behind her, she set out for a glorious week in Florida. She had no doubt that, by the time she returned, her mother would be over her peeve.

## Chapter Ten

The sky was brightening with the first faint rays of a rose-colored dawn as Eric and Connie walked hand in hand along the Florida beach. The deep-blue waters of the ocean blended with the still-darkened sky and lapped at a white, sandy shore. Connie stopped to wiggle her toes in the wet sand and let the foam from the ebbing tide rise up around her ankles. Her hair was damp with sea spray, her face glowing with happiness. "This is absolutely the most heavenly place I've ever seen," she said, smiling up at Eric.

He bent his head to kiss her lightly. "It's a beautiful place, all right. But as far as I'm concerned, it isn't where we are that's so special; it's being with you."

Connie slid an arm around his waist, and they stood watching the motion of the sea. "It truly has been

134

wonderful, being together like this. I can't thank your parents enough for making it possible.''

''They've loved having us here. And they've loved getting to know you. They're convinced you're the best thing that has ever happened to our family.''

''They're wonderful people. I never imagined anyone could be as kind and thoughtful.''

She had to search for words to express her feelings. The visit with the Lindstroms had been, from its beginning, the happiest of experiences. Arthur Lindstrom was an impressive man in his mid-sixties with his son's clean-cut good looks and calm self-assurance. Iris Lindstrom was a slim, attractive woman with a vibrant personality, boundless interests, and a youthful outlook that belied her years. The two of them had welcomed Connie with an enthusiastic approval that had at once made her feel welcome and at ease.

While the Lindstroms asked no questions about the young couple's plans, they made it clear that they understood Connie was special to Eric when they proudly introduced her to their friends in the retirement village where they lived. Iris had entertained for her with a luncheon at the club that served the seaside community of townhouses. The Lindstroms had held a small dinner party to introduce Eric and Connie to their closer friends. No one could have offered a warmer reception, and Connie already felt a real kinship with both Arthur and Iris.

And yet, Eric's parents had not monopolized their

son's time but had continued with their own activities, thoughtfully leaving the young couple long hours for themselves and providing them with a car so that they could sight-see as much as they liked. They had sunned on the beach, driven along the coast to visit nearby towns, dined at restaurants the Lindstroms recommended. That morning, they had arisen before dawn to enjoy a stroll on the beach at sunrise.

Connie rested her head contentedly against Eric's shoulder as they admired the rose-tinged sea. "I didn't imagine anything could be so perfect as this week has been. I'll never forget it," she said softly.

"I hope not. In fact, I'm planning a lot more just like it." He paused to brush his lips against her cheek. "As a matter of fact, there's another place I want you to see. It isn't too far up the coast from here, and I thought we might drive up there tomorrow."

"What kind of a place is it?" Connie asked, her curiosity aroused.

Eric shook his head mysteriously. "I'm not going to tell you anything about it in advance. I'd rather you formed your own unbiased opinion."

In spite of her pleas, he refused to answer any questions. Her curiosity was still unsatisfied when they set out on their trip very early the following morning. Their drive took them along the coast, and there was an unending procession of interesting sights to claim her attention. She settled back to enjoy herself, content to wait until Eric was ready to reveal his surprise.

It was midmorning when they arrived at their destination, a lovely, sleepy little town named San Gabriel, which was located a short distance inland from the main highway. Eric made a leisurely tour through the quiet streets, visiting various points of interest before he stopped in front of a cluster of low white buildings near the edge of town. Centered by a palmetto-shaded plaza, the complex was identified by a stone marker at the edge of a narrow driveway that wound through the grounds. Connie turned to him, puzzled, as she read the marker. "This says Merrill College. Is there something special about it?"

He nodded. "I was a student here for a while. It's a small school, but it offers a fine curriculum in music and art."

"So you brought me here to see your old school," she said with an indulgent smile as she studied the buildings with heightened interest. "This is certainly a nice location for a school, as close to the ocean as it is. I imagine you got in some good playtime at the beach while you were here."

"Both the school and the town have their attractions." He lingered a moment before he drove off, circling through the streets to slow down in front of another, larger building. "This is one of the attractions. It looks a lot different from the one you're used to and is much smaller, but it's a surprisingly good hospital. As a matter of fact, it has quite a good physical-therapy department. I thought you might like to stop and take a look at it.''

Without waiting for Connie's answer, he found a parking place. Puzzled by his insistence, she accompanied him to a side door of the hospital, which she discovered to be the entrance to an outpatient treatment facility. Seeming well acquainted with his surroundings, he led her directly to the physical-therapy section.

"I'm amazed that a small town like this can support a service of this kind," she said when she saw the size and quality of the treatment area.

"The hospital draws from a large area and doesn't overreach itself. It doesn't try to duplicate the special facilities of a large city hospital, but the services it offers are very good."

Connie's curiosity was now totally aroused. "How do you know so much about the PT department?"

"Because I spent some time here as an outpatient when I was a student at Merrill." He looked around him with interest. "Of course, they've improved the place considerably since then. I understand that they're well funded, and they seem to have made the most of it."

"Much to the advantage of the patients, I'm sure."

"Definitely."

A question stirred in her mind. "Why are you showing me this, Eric?"

"There's one more place I want you to see before I answer that question," he answered mysteriously.

Taking her by the hand, he led her to the car and drove back to the highway, refusing to reveal their destination.

A short time later they arrived at a real estate development close to the seashore. Eric parked in front of one house that was being offered for sale. Ignoring Connie's questions, he took her inside where they made a tour of it.

He waited until they had finished their inspection before he turned—a bit anxiously, she thought—to ask, "How do you like it?"

"I think it's perfect," she exclaimed with pleasure. "It's an absolute dream."

She was indeed enchanted by the house. Designed in the style of a beach cottage, it was perfectly planned. Its large, roomy living area opened onto a sun room and outdoor deck. A compact kitchen was equipped with the latest appliances and an inviting dining nook that overlooked a palmetto-shaded garden. There was a spacious bedroom, adjoined by a cozy sitting room and luxurious dressing room and bath. A small but private guest suite completed the main floor.

The main attraction of the house, however, was the single room that occupied its second floor. Bright, airy, and spacious, the big room was perfectly designed to serve as a studio. Its wide windows admitted a maximum of light as well as providing a spectacular view of the nearby ocean.

A glimmer of suspicion stirred in Connie's mind.

"Why are you showing me this, Eric? What's this all about?"

"It's part of an explanation. I had a special reason for bringing you to Florida, you see. I wanted you to discover for yourself what it would be like to live here."

"I don't understand," she said, now totally mystified.

He studied her expression intently as he answered, "What it comes down to, Connie, is that you and I have a decision to make. I've had one of those offers that's too good to refuse. It happened rather suddenly, and I only got the details worked out a couple of weeks ago. Since then I've been setting things up in San Gabriel for you to see. I thought you would understand better if you knew firsthand what I was talking about."

"You've been offered a job here?"

"That's part of it. What has happened is that my Lindy strip is going to be run daily from now on."

"But that's wonderful, Eric."

"I think so too, of course. But it's going to mean a good bit more work for me and will mean that I'm not going to be able to teach as I have in the past. I've had a standing offer for a while to teach a course in cartooning at Merrill College, and this seemed the perfect time to take advantage of it. The college can give me the flexibility in time I need, and they seem to feel that in return I can offer them a course that will enhance their art program."

"As well as the attraction of your name," Connie said, beginning to understand.

"They seem to think I have something to offer that would attract certain students. In turn, they can give me some facilities I need. It's a golden opportunity for me, but it's one I want you to share with me. I'm hoping you'll agree to come along and start a new life with me."

"You're asking me to. . . ." Connie faltered, too breathless to continue.

"To marry me. I haven't made a secret of how I feel about you. I've known from the day I first met you that you were the woman for me, and I know we can have a good life together. I was waiting until I thought you were ready to make a decision, but the offer from the syndicate speeded things up. We'd need to be settled in here as soon as possible so that I'll be ready to start teaching in September."

"That's less than three months from now," Connie exclaimed.

"There's time enough if we get busy right away. The main question is whether you think you can be happy married to me."

"I'm happy just being with you," she said softly.

"But are you ready to spend your life with me?"

A yearning appeared in his eyes, and as Connie gazed up at him, she knew without question that this was the only man she wanted to spend her life with and that he was offering her the only kind of life she wanted to live. "Oh, yes," she whispered. "In fact, I can't imagine any kind of life at all without you."

He gave a contented sigh as he gathered her in her arms. "I do love you, Connie, and I'll do my best to make you happy."

She raised her lips to his, offering him her life and her heart and her soul. How could she possibly hope to be any happier than she was at this moment?

The rest of the day passed in a whirlwind of activity. Eric made an offer to purchase the house. They returned to Merrill College, where Connie viewed the facilities of the school and met several administrators and faculty members. Last of all, they paid a second visit to the local hospital where, Eric confessed, he had made arrangements for Connie to talk to the director of Rehabilitation Services.

Knowing she wouldn't want to abandon her own career, he had determined in advance that the department was in need of an experienced physical therapist. Leaving nothing to chance, he had paved the way for an interview for her if she wanted it.

By the time they began their return drive to his parents' home, Eric had signed a contract with the college, they had begun the paperwork on the purchase of a house, and Connie had begun negotiations for a job at the hospital.

Iris and Arthur were delighted by the news and offered their enthusiastic support. Eric and Connie spent their last two days of vacation reveling in the joy of being together and celebrating their exciting new commitments. By the time they returned home on Sunday night, tanned and glowing with happiness, they had already embarked on their plans for a glorious future together.

On Monday morning Connie gave notice to Dr. Foster. While he expressed his deep regret at her resignation, he heartily endorsed her decision to marry Eric and offered them his sincere best wishes. He also promised to supply the hospital in San Gabriel with his highest recommendation of Connie's professional qualifications.

Gena Farrell was, of course, ecstatic. "It's fantastic," she exclaimed. "Imagine having an exciting new job, your very own dreamhouse, and most of all marrying a man as totally terrific as Eric. You've really hit the jackpot, Connie."

"Don't forget a wonderful new set of in-laws. Eric's parents are super. I'm very lucky to have their full approval."

"They're lucky too. You're a fine person, and you'll make Eric a wonderful wife." Gena gave Connie an affectionate hug. "You deserve every bit of the happiness that's coming to you."

Warmed by the good wishes of her friends and co-workers, Connie was in the best of moods when she met Eric after work. Having arrived in town very late the previous night, they had postponed the announcement of their plans until the family could be together. At her request the family members were already gathering by the time she arrived with Eric at the D'Angelo home.

Although obviously not surprised, her brothers and sisters-in-law received the news with unrestrained enthusiasm. Janice and Milly responded with affectionate hugs for both Eric and Connie. Joe and Vic expressed their approval with hearty slaps on Eric's back and dire warnings concerning their sister's temper. Frankie, with a pleased grin, draped a comradely arm over Eric's shoulders and pronounced, "It'll be great to have you as a brother-in-law. Welcome to the family if you can stand it."

Even Sam offered his endorsement of their plans. Although there was a trace of regret in his expression and the glint of a tear in his eye, his sincerity was evident as he clasped Eric's hand. "I won't say I'm not sorry to give her up, but she couldn't have chosen a better man. I know you'll be good to my little girl."

"I'll never give you any cause to worry about her," Eric promised. There was no questioning the earnestness of his pledge. And as Connie recognized the bond which had at that moment formed between the two most important men in her life, her happiness spilled over.

There was, however, one member of the D'Angelo family who failed to join in the celebration of the occasion. Stella, while she voiced no disapproval, listened without comment to her daughter's plans. She said nothing while Connie explained about Eric's good fortune with his cartoon strip; she made no comment about their new jobs in Florida. It was only during an excited description of the house where they would live that Stella finally spoke. "I've heard about Florida, and it's no place to live," she announced with finality. "They've got alligators there—and bugs as big as toads."

"That's not true, Mama. Florida is as safe as any other state. And it's a beautiful place to live."

"I know what I know," Stella retorted, refusing to be convinced. "I've seen pictures of alligators in people's backyards. And the sharks come right up to the beach. It's no place for you to be, Connie. You won't like it, I can tell you."

Connie groaned in annoyance. Trust Mama to dampen their pleasure with her gloomy outlook. "You don't know anything at all about Florida. You're just prejudiced because you don't want me to move away."

Stella didn't answer. Nor did she join again in the conversation. She sat, stone-faced, while Sam called in an order for pizza. "None for me. I don't feel so good," she said, rising heavily from her chair. She went to her room and didn't appear again.

Connie was bitterly disappointed and deeply hurt that her mother would selfishly spoil this important moment. Although she tried to hide her feelings from Eric, she didn't succeed. Before he left, he held her close to him in a comforting embrace. "Don't be upset, Connie. You knew it would take a little while for her to get used to the idea."

"But it's so unfair of her. It's not right for her to ruin things for us."

"She can't spoil this time for us unless we let her. She'll come around eventually. You'll see."

But Connie had her doubts. She knew how stubborn her mother could be when she set her head to it.

The next morning Connie's fears were confirmed. She was dressing for work when her brother Frankie knocked on her bedroom door. "Pop says you should come and take a look at Mama. Something has happened to her," he said. "She says she's sick and she can't get out of bed."

The doctors at City Medical Center were baffled. Although a battery of tests revealed no specific cause for her ailment, Stella insisted that she was a sick woman. "I hurt," she declared and adamantly refused to leave her bed.

The orthopedic specialist, finding no evidence of any physical dysfunction, suggested that an exercise program might be beneficial. Dr. Foster tactfully concurred in the opinion. Stella responded with an indignant protest. "How am I supposed to do exercises when my back is killing me?"

Connie tried her best to explain how a program of physical therapy could help, but her mother refused to be convinced. At last, in desperation, Connie sought the advice of neurosurgeon Ross McKinnon, the husband of her former roommate, Amanda Summers McKinnon. After ordering a series of tests that revealed no neurological problems, Ross agreed with his colleagues.

"In my opinion, your mother is suffering from lack of physical activity. She needs to get out of bed and get some exercise," Ross reported with his usual bluntness.

"But what about her pain? It's been going on for months now, and there's bound to be an explanation."

"I'm sure there is, but I'm not the doctor to supply it. I don't suggest that your mother isn't experiencing the pain. I just question the cause of it. You know, it's possible that stress or perhaps psychological problems may be the cause of her symptoms."

"If you're telling me we should consult a psychiatrist, I don't think she would ever agree. She'd go into orbit at the very suggestion," Connie said in frustration.

Ross gave her an encouraging smile. "Let's hope it won't be necessary. Maybe we can get her to cooperate in an exercise program and see if it'll do the trick. In the meantime, you might talk to Amanda and see if she has any ideas."

Connie was heartened by his suggestion. Her friend

Amanda was a skilled psychologist who was very good at getting through to people. If all else failed, maybe she could find a way to help Stella.

In the meantime, the only thing to do was insist that Stella follow the exercise program the doctors had prescribed. With a daughter who could work with her at home, she had no excuse for refusing. But however she had to do it, Connie was determined to get Stella well again. What was the good of being a physical therapist if you couldn't help your own mother?

Stella, still complaining, was released from the hospital. Connie determinedly set up a program of home therapy, putting aside time every day to work with her mother. If their preparations for their move to Florida were interrupted, she and Eric would simply have to make the best of it. The sooner Stella got back on her feet, the sooner they could get on with their wedding plans.

While Eric was less confident of Stella's speedy recovery than Connie, he agreed that she had to do her best to help her mother. He didn't complain when the responsibility interfered with their time to be together. Leaving Connie free to concentrate on Stella's treatment, he moved ahead with the arrangements for their move.

It was a trying time for both of them. The happiness they should have been sharing was shadowed by uncertainty. With little time for each other and even less time to attend to their own affairs, they both became increasingly pressured as the month of June passed with noticeable lack of improvement in Stella's condition. July advanced with few wedding plans made and no provision at all for moving into the house in San Gabriel. Now frantic, Connie concentrated all her attention on her mother's treatment while Eric made a trip to Florida to attend to his now-pressing business there.

He returned on an evening late in July to find Connie exhausted from her day's work at the hospital and a long, unproductive session with Stella. It was almost ten o'clock by the time they could snatch a moment to be alone together.

They retreated to the front porch and sank down on the porch swing, both of them tired and dejected. Battling fatigue, discouragement, and the oppressive summer heat, neither of them spoke for a while. It was Eric who at last broke the silence to ask brusquely, "Why didn't you tell me you haven't given the hospital in San Gabriel a final acceptance on their offer? I found out today that you haven't committed to a definite starting date."

"I didn't mention it to you because I thought matters would straighten out soon, but things here are still so unsettled that I was reluctant to set a specific date," Connie explained uncomfortably. "I kept thinking each day that I would know more, but so far nothing has changed."

He frowned. "You're not being fair to the hospital.

They have a right to know what you plan to do. For that matter, it's not fair to you and me, either, because we've got plans that are affected too. If you're having trouble making a decision, you should have told me.''

''I haven't any problem with my decision. It's just that nothing is turning out the way we planned.'' Connie gave a disheartened sigh. ''I'm getting really discouraged, Eric. I'm getting absolutely nowhere with Mama.''

He shifted restlessly in the porch swing, leaning forward to rest his elbows on his knees. ''I'm as concerned about your mother as you are, but time is running out for us. You've given all the time you can to Stella, and we have to move on with our own lives.''

''But how can I just go off and leave her in this condition?'' Connie appealed to him. ''I don't know how Pop can possibly manage without me.''

''Your parents will manage the same way they would if you had already moved to Florida. Face it, Connie. Sooner or later they're going to have to learn to get along without you. You're not a child anymore; you're a woman with a right to a life of her own. We're talking about our future now, and we have to get on with it.''

''And we will. It's just that I could leave with a clear conscience if I knew Mama was going to be all right, and I'm sure I could get her over this spell if only we had a little more time.''

''There isn't any more time,'' Eric said impatiently. ''I'm committed to start teaching in barely six weeks.

We have to be moved into a house in Florida by then, you have to start a new job—assuming you still want it—and somehow along the way we have to attend to the minor detail of getting married.''

In the face of the formidable obstacles that confronted them, Connie's courage deserted her. "I don't see how we can do it,'' she said with fading hope.

Eric ran a hand through his hair in frustration. "We have to do it. We can't put things off any longer. We have no choice but to stop wasting time and get on with the things we have to do.''

Connie sat silently, seeing no solution to their impossible dilemma. At last she made a hesitant suggestion. "Maybe you should just go on to Florida. You could be getting the house settled while I finish up with Mama here. I could follow later when things are under control.''

"What about your job? You can't expect the hospital to hold it for you much longer. It doesn't matter to me whether you work at all, of course, but I thought your career was important to you.''

"I love my work, and I don't want to give it up. Under the circumstances, though, I guess I'll have to wait and look for a job after I can get settled in Florida.''

"And where would you look for a job if the hospital fills the place there? There aren't too many jobs open for physical therapists in a little place like San Gabriel.''

"I'll just have to worry about that when the time comes. I don't know what else I can do," Connie said miserably.

He cast a long, measuring glance at her. There was an edge to his voice when he said, "You do have a choice, but I guess it comes down to whether you're ready to make it. It seems to me that what you have to decide is how important to you it is to marry me."

"You know what I want, Eric. It's just a matter of delaying our plans for a little while."

"For how long? A month—six months—a year?"

"Of course not. Just until Mama is up and able to manage without me."

He shook his head unhappily. "I don't think so. However long you stay here, nothing is going to change. The fact is that your mother doesn't want you to marry anyone. She doesn't want to give you up. She'll always find some way to keep you with her if you let her."

"That's not fair, Eric. She can't help it if she's sick. Surely it isn't asking too much for us to delay our plans for just a little while until she's well again."

Eric said nothing but sat staring out into the summer night. After a long silence he turned to her, his expression desolate but resigned. "We both have to make a choice, Connie. You have a right to make yours, and I guess I've already made mine. I've made commitments that I intend to honor, and I'm going to move to Florida on schedule. Either you love me enough to come with me and make a new life with me, or your family takes first place and you stay here. It's as simple as that."

"It isn't that simple," Connie said, stricken. "If you cared for me enough, you wouldn't ask me to make such a choice. You'd be willing to wait until I'm free of my responsibilities here."

"I'm willing to wait for you, but I'm not going to drift along pretending," he said quietly. "I'll rent an apartment in San Gabriel and get on with what I have to do, but I'm not going to move into a house you'll never live in or count on plans that may never come to pass. Until you get things worked out and are ready to make a commitment to me, I'll have to get on with my life without you."

Connie stared at him, shocked, unwilling to believe he could care so little for her feelings. Out of selfishness, he was willing to throw away everything they had planned. The wonderful life, the challenging job, the beautiful house were vanishing simply because he wasn't willing to make a simple compromise. She fought back tears as she said, heartbroken, "If you cared for me as you say you do, you'd be willing to help me work this out. If you loved me, you'd be patient for a little while."

"It isn't a question of my loving you. The question is how much you love me. More than anything in the world, I want us to be together and have all the happiness I know we could have. But if it turns out that you don't love me enough to commit to a future with me, I have no choice but to start getting used to a life without you." His expression was bleak but determined. "You have to make a choice too, Connie. Let me know when you decide what you want to do."

He rose from the porch swing and with a last, sad glance at her walked to his car. She sat motionless, watching him drive away. It was only when the glow of the headlights had faded into the darkness that she finally accepted the reality that he was gone. Only then did she understand that all her dreams had crashed around her and she had lost him. Bitterly she buried her face in her hands and wept.

*Chapter Eleven*

T he next few days were miserable for Connie while she waited for Eric to call. She refused to get in touch with him. After all, it was he who had refused to compromise. She couldn't believe that, as soon as he realized how selfish he was being, he wouldn't agree to some reasonable accommodation. With a little cooperation they could surely work through this foolish disagreement.

After several days passed without word from him, however, her confidence began to waver. A small doubt began to grow into a real fear. Maybe Eric wasn't going to change his mind. Maybe he really did intend to go on with his life without her.

Feeling hurt and dejected, she went despondently about her work in the PT Department. A tight-lipped

Gena Farrell watched her with concern. Although Gena asked no questions, there was no doubt that she suspected the reason for her friend's unhappiness.

At last, unable to bear the silence any longer, she intercepted Connie in the hallway at noon one day. Holding out two paper-wrapped sandwiches and two canned cold drinks, she said forcefully, "At the risk of meddling, I'm going to insist that you and I take a lunch break and have a talk. What good is a friend if she can't be of any help when you've got problems? And if I ever saw anybody with a problem, it's you."

Connie reluctantly followed Gena to a shady park bench in the courtyard outside the PT department. There wasn't any help her friend could give her. There was only one person who could solve her problem, and apparently he wasn't willing to do it.

Undeterred, Gena handed out the sandwiches and drinks and stated bluntly, "This has gone on long enough, so let's hear it. I want to know what's gone wrong between you and Eric."

"What's gone wrong is that Eric is a totally selfish man," Connie answered resentfully.

"He hasn't been up to now. What's happened to change him?"

In spite of her efforts to control it, Connie's chin quivered. "He's calling off our wedding."

Gena looked at her skeptically. "I won't believe that for a second. Loving you as much as he does, he would never do that."

"He might as well have. He says he has commitments he has to meet and he's going to move to Florida in time to meet them. He knows I can't possibly leave now, but he won't even consider going ahead and getting settled without me. He says I can either come with him or he'll move into an apartment and give up the house."

"But what about your job? Don't you have to start to work at the hospital there pretty soon?"

"I haven't been able to set a date because I don't know when I'll be able to go to work. If the hospital has to go ahead and hire someone else, there's nothing I can do about it."

"But you've already given your notice here," Gena said, now concerned. "What will you do if you lose out on the job in Florida?"

"I guess that's just a chance I'll have to take. Either there will be a job for me when I can get to Florida, or I'll have to work out something else."

"But surely you're not seriously considering postponing your wedding!"

"Eric isn't giving me a choice," Connie said bitterly. "He says either we go ahead with our plans and move to Florida together, or we put everything on hold until I get things worked out. He knows very well that with things the way they are at home, there's no way I can leave here right now. But he isn't willing to move into the house in San Gabriel and let me follow whenever I can."

"Maybe he thinks you'll never get there," Gena suggested, leveling a meaningful glance at her friend.

"That's exactly what he thinks, and it's what hurts so much. He doesn't trust me to keep my promise. He's making me choose between him and my responsibility to my parents when he knows I don't really have a choice. He's blaming Mama for being sick, and it isn't fair."

"I see." Gena nibbled slowly on her sandwich for a few moments before she ventured a tentative question. "Is it really so important that you stay on with your mother? After all, there's really nothing more that you can do. About all she can do now is get the proper medical advice, and she can hire someone to take care of the house until she gets well. She might even recover more quickly if you weren't around to do for her."

"But it would be cruel to just go off and leave her," Connie exclaimed, aghast at the thought.

"You're going to have to leave home sometime. Why not now, before you mess up your own life?"

Connie shook her head vehemently. "Mama gave up her life for her children, and I can't refuse to help her now that she needs someone to look after her."

"Your mother didn't give up her life for you. She lived the way she chose," Gena objected. "Now it's your turn to choose the life you want to live."

"I can't turn my back on my mother. I couldn't live with myself if I abandoned her," Connie said with finality.

Gena's expression was thoughtful. "Has it occurred to you that maybe Eric feels that you're abandoning him?"

"He knows that isn't the case. I'm just asking him to put things on hold for a little while so that I can repay my mother for all she's done for me. It isn't a lot to ask, you know. We've got our whole lives ahead of us to do the things we want to do."

"Maybe. Maybe not. Life doesn't offer any certainties. I just hope you don't look back and find out you've thrown away something wonderful that you can never get back."

Having offered her opinion, Gena rose from the bench and dumped her sandwich bag and drink can in the trash bins provided for them. She said nothing more to Connie as they started back to the PT department. But Connie felt a little shiver of apprehension as she closed the iron gate on the courtyard. Looking back at the little garden and recalling the day she had first seen Eric sleeping there on the park bench, an inconsolable sorrow engulfed her. What would she do if it was really over between them? How could she bear it if she lost him for good?

Shaken by her conversation with Gena, Connie now waited with a feverish anxiety for Eric to call. Time was rapidly slipping away, and the moment was fast approaching when there would be no turning back. When several more days passed without word from him, she began to despair. She was now beset by the haunting fear that maybe he wasn't going to call.

There was no way she could hide her unhappiness from her family. Although no one asked questions, their polite silence told her that all of them knew something was wrong. Even Stella watched her intently as they went through their nightly treatment sessions without mention of Eric.

Frankie finally made an attempt to talk to her. He followed her to the front porch one hot, sultry night to find her leaning against a column, staring disconsolately into the darkness. Dropping an arm around her shoulders, he said awkwardly, ''I don't know what's going on with you and Eric, but if there's anything I can do to help, I'd like to try. I thought you two had something pretty special going for you.''

Connie gave him a dismal smile. ''There's nothing anyone can do. This is just something Eric and I have to work out.''

''I hope it hasn't got anything to do with Mama's being sick.''

''It isn't Mama who's to blame.''

''I hope not, because you shouldn't let her problems come between the two of you. Eric's a great guy, and I'd hate to see things go wrong for you.'' He gave her a clumsy hug. ''Don't let things around here keep you from doing what it takes to get back on track. Pop and I can manage.''

Sam also had something to say about Connie's unhappy situation. The next morning, while she was preparing her mother's breakfast, he looked up from his morning paper to direct a worried glance at her. "You can tell me it's none of my business, but I hope things aren't getting out of hand between you and Eric," he said hesitantly. "I know I haven't always had the best things to say about him, but I've come to think a lot of him, and I'd hate to think you two were letting other people's problems cause trouble for you. Your mother and I have managed well enough in our time, and we can do it again."

Connie was touched that her father and brother were concerned for her, but she knew that their well-meant assurances weren't realistic. It was easy to talk about managing without her, but doing it was another matter. There was no way the two of them could run the house and look after a woman's needs. In spite of their good intentions, they were as impractical as Eric.

Their concern did prompt Connie to realize that perhaps she was being unrealistic too. Simply waiting around for her mother to get well wasn't going to help any of them. Since none of her mother's treatments had worked so far, maybe she needed to look for a different approach. Ross McKinnon believed that Stella's problems weren't physical. If so, it was time to find out what was causing them. Maybe it was time to take Ross's suggestion and have a talk with his wife, Amanda.

Psychologist Amanda McKinnon, Connie's former

roommate, had left City Medical Center the previous year to take a job as a counselor at a family-services clinic. Although she and Connie saw each other less frequently than they would have liked, they still were close friends. If there was any way to discover what was wrong with Stella, Amanda would do her best to find it.

A telephone call prompted Amanda's immediate response, and she arranged a meeting with Connie after work the same day. When Connie arrived at the McKinnons' apartment, her friend was waiting with a pitcher of iced tea and a plate of cookies.

"What you need is one of our heart-to-hearts," she said after a single glance at Connie's woebegone face. "You helped me when I had my troubles with Ross, and now it's my turn to help you. Let's talk this over and see what we can come up with."

Seated on a comfortable sofa and sipping on tall glasses of iced tea, the two of them slipped at once into the comradely relationship they had enjoyed when they were roommates. Amanda's sympathetic understanding opened the floodgates to Connie's unhappiness, and her troubles poured out.

"What hurts so much is that Eric doesn't care about my feelings," she finished. "He doesn't care if Mama's sick, and he won't even consider any kind of compromise. He insists that I do what he wants when he knows it's not possible."

"Why do you think he's doing this?" Amanda asked.

"Because he isn't thinking of anybody but himself. He wants me to go to Florida with him right now, regardless of anybody else."

"Why is it so important to him that you come with him now?"

Connie faltered. "He thinks I won't come if he goes on without me."

"But you do plan to go?"

"Of course. As soon as Mama's well."

"Then maybe we need to consider why your mother isn't getting any better," Amanda said calmly. She set down her glass of tea, leaned back against the arm of the sofa, and began a matter-of-fact assessment of Stella's case. "Ross has given me her medical background. You tell me that the suggested treatments aren't working. In your professional opinion, why do you think your mother isn't improving?"

Connie shrugged helplessly. "She just isn't responding."

"But why isn't she responding? Doesn't she want to get well?"

"Of course she does!" Connie exclaimed irritably. "Why wouldn't she want to get well?"

Amanda leveled a kind but incisive glance at Connie. "Maybe that's a question you ought to be asking yourself."

Connie was taken aback. There was a suggestion in

Amanda's remark from which she instantly retreated. "Surely you're not suggesting that Mama is faking. Her pain isn't imagined. It's real."

"I'm sure it is, Connie. Or at least she thinks it is."

"But you're not convinced she's really sick," Connie said, instantly rejecting the possibility.

"Whether I'm convinced or not isn't at issue. What is important is how Stella feels. Sometimes when we have very strong wishes, our minds influence our bodies. Maybe this is what's happening to her."

Connie shook her head vehemently. "If you're saying Mama is making herself sick because she doesn't want me to leave home, I can't go along with you. She would never do such a thing."

"Most likely she wouldn't even be aware of it. Think about it, Connie," Amanda urged gently. "Your mother loves you, and she wouldn't deliberately hurt you, but hasn't she always resisted when you've tried to leave home?"

"Mama just likes to have her family around her. She can't be blamed for that," Connie defended her mother.

"No more than you can be blamed for wanting to be with her," Amanda agreed.

A glimmer of suspicion began to form in Connie's mind as she perceived that she had just been skillfully led through a counseling session. "Don't play games with me, Amanda. You've got something on your mind, and I want to hear it. Tell me exactly what you think is wrong.''

''What I think isn't important. What *is* important is that you understand how *you* feel—about Eric and about your mother and about yourself. Until you're clear about your own feelings, you're not going to be able to make the decision Eric is asking you to make.''

''If he loved me enough, he wouldn't ask me to make it,'' Connie insisted.

''But don't you see that this is the very reason he is forcing you to a decision? Maybe he feels that if you loved *him* enough, there would be only one decision you'd be willing to make.''

''It isn't that simple,'' Connie protested in frustration. ''What about Mama?''

''If you decide to go with Eric, she'll simply have to accept it—just as he'll have to accept it if you choose to stay here. But the real decision is up to you, Connie. You have to decide whether it's more important to you to be your mother's daughter or Eric's wife.''

Connie drove home, distracted. Her meeting with Amanda had left her troubled and confused. Instead of the clear-cut answer she had been seeking, she had uncovered a whole new set of uncertainties. Uncomfortably, too, she was now beset by a growing doubt. Was it possible that it wasn't Eric who was being unreasonable? Was it she who was making a mistake?

\* \* \*

After her talk with Amanda, Connie was more confused than ever. She seemed incapable of making any
kind of decision. She knew that, if she wasn't going
to accept a position at the hospital in San Gabriel, she
was obligated to let them know of her decision at once.
It was equally as urgent to speak to Dr. Foster about
her job here at City Medical Center. If she wasn't going
to be leaving, she needed to let him know it.

And yet she wasn't ready to give up on all the lovely
dreams she and Eric had shared. The thought that he
would be going on to San Gabriel with no understanding between them that she would ever join him was
more than she could bear. If only he would call, they
might still salvage at least some of their hopes. Yet
his ominous silence told her that there would be no
compromise. With every hour that passed, her dreams
were fading. Every day brought her closer to the time
when he would be gone—perhaps for good.

Determinedly, she shelved her unhappy thoughts
when she went to work the next day. Her years of rigid
training served her well. She was able to suppress her
troubled emotions through most of the day, but early
in the afternoon they burst from control when a former
patient paid her a visit.

She was leaving the PT department to attend an
afternoon meeting when she found Rob Nelson waiting
for her in the reception room. "Hi, Miss D'Angelo.
Remember me?" he called out to her.

The sight of Eric's former student brought back a

rush of memories. Memories of the day she had met Eric, the happy times they had shared, the pain of their parting. It took a supreme effort to manage a faint smile for Rob. "How could I forget you? We don't get star basketball players in here every day. I take it, since I haven't seen you recently, that your knee isn't giving you any more trouble."

"It's completely well. My doctor says I'm ready to play basketball again. By fall I ought to be ready to go out for the school team."

"If you work back into play gradually, you should do fine," Connie agreed.

"That's what Mr. Lindstrom says. He's given me a schedule to follow."

Connie felt a pang of regret at the mention of Eric's name. She covered it as best she could and said, "I hope you'll take his advice."

"You don't have to warn me. I don't want to end up with a knee like his. He's really having his troubles."

Connie's attention sharpened. "What kind of trouble?"

"He's on crutches. He hurt his knee again and can barely get around."

"What happened to his knee?" she asked in alarm.

"He hurt it some way loading boxes."

"How long has this been going on?"

"Maybe a week or so. I found out about it when he called me to ask if I could get some of the guys from school to come by his place and help him pack. I guess it's been really hard for him, what with him trying to move. I told him not to worry, because we can get him packed up and all. But I don't know what he's going to do when he gets to Florida. It looks like he may be laid up for a while.''

''Surely he isn't planning to go ahead with a move,'' Connie exclaimed. ''His knee needs attention—maybe even surgery.''

''He doesn't have any choice, because he has to get out of his apartment. He says he'll get his knee taken care of when he gets moved. Right now his biggest problem is driving his car to Florida.''

''There's no way he can make a drive that long with his knee in the shape it's in,'' Connie protested.

''He says he'll worry about it later.''

Her temper exploded. What kind of fool thing was Eric planning to do? There was no way he could drive to Florida alone and manage a move by himself. And what would he do about his knee when he got there? There was no way he could get the proper treatment and still teach and meet the deadlines for his cartoon strips. She couldn't understand what he was thinking about. It was absurd for him to even consider striking out on his own with no one to help him.

Mumbling an incoherent excuse, she wheeled away from Rob and marched to the nearest telephone. Angrily she put in a call to Eric's apartment. When he answered on the first ring, she said indignantly, ''I'm on my way over there, Eric Lindstrom. Don't you move until I get there!''

Slamming down the telephone, she left the hospital without a thought for the meeting she was scheduled to attend. As she drove across town to Eric's apartment, she was furious to think he had let his stubborn pride get him into this situation. How could he sit there all alone and helpless and never let her know what had happened to him?

By the time she approached the door to his apartment, her anger had begun to give way to concern. Fearfully she wondered what condition she would find him in. Her anxiety only increased when, in response to her knock on his door, a wan voice called out, ''It's open.''

She stepped inside to see him seated in a lounge chair. His leg, the knee lumpily wrapped in elastic bandages, was propped on an ottoman. Wearing wrinkled shorts and a T-shirt, his hair tousled and a light beard covering his chin, he presented a bleak sight. The little crinkles of fatigue around his eyes told her at once that he was in pain.

''You look awful!'' she exclaimed at the sight of him.

His lips curved in a weak smile as his glance traveled over her trim figure. ''You look pretty good to me.''

She ran to his side and knelt beside the ottoman. Unwrapping the bandage that braced his knee, she exclaimed in dismay. The knee, swollen and discolored, was even worse than she had imagined. "What have you done to yourself?" she demanded.

He shrugged apologetically. "I twisted it loading boxes into the van."

"Why didn't you tell me about it? You know I would have come to help you if you had called."

He reached out to touch her cheek longingly. "I kept hoping that maybe you'd call me."

Her anger flared. "So you just sat here, too stubborn to give in and ask for help."

"I hoped I wouldn't have to. I hoped that maybe you cared enough about me to want to see me as much as I wanted to see you." His eyes drank in the sight of her; his fingers caressed her face, lightly tracing her lips. "I've missed you so much, Connie—more than you can ever imagine."

"So much that you never once gave in and called me," she accused him bitterly. "Was your pride that important to you?"

"It wasn't pride. It was desperation. It was the only way I knew to make you see what we were about to lose." His expression was pleading, revealing his hurt. "I had to hope you couldn't face getting along without me any more than I could get along without you. I don't know how it's been for you, but I've never been so miserable in my life as I have these last two weeks."

As she heard the longing in his voice and saw the pain in his eyes, Connie's heart filled with a fierce, protective love for him. From somewhere deep inside her, her pent-up longing burst free. "I don't ever want to go through this again. I don't ever want to be away from you," she whispered. "Wherever we have to go, I'm going with you."

Somehow she slid onto his lap, and his arms closed around her. All the feelings she had suppressed rushed out as she clung to him, sharing the sweetness of their love as he kissed her. And as she nestled close to him, all her doubts slipped away. She knew without question that this was where she belonged, the place where she wanted to be. This was the man she had given her heart to, the man she would love for the rest of her life.

Suddenly she remembered his injured knee. She sat up and exclaimed remorsefully, "I'm so sorry. Your knee is bound to be hurting."

He answered with a blissful smile. "Not to worry. I've never had anything hurt so good in my life."

"But we haven't got a moment to waste," she protested. "We have to get busy and treat that knee."

"It's been sore for a couple of weeks already. A few more minutes won't make a difference," he said, refusing to release her.

"Oh, yes, it will," she said, jumping to her feet. "We have to get you up and around. In less than a month we've got to be married and moved to Florida."

It was close to nine o'clock when they finally settled down on the sofa. Eric's knee, now elevated on a chair, already showed improvement, thanks to Connie's ministrations. Reinforced by the supper she had prepared, he leaned back comfortably against a sofa cushion, delighted with their accomplishments. After dozens of telephone calls, their plans were back on track.

Both of them were scheduled to go to work in San Gabriel on the first of September. Arrangements had been made for the treatment of Eric's knee as soon as they arrived there. A moving company had been hired and a simple wedding planned. They had a hectic month ahead of them, but their move would be accomplished on schedule.

Connie was making a final check of their list of things to be done when she noticed an omission. "We've got to call the moving company back!" she exclaimed. "We'll need to tell them where to take the furniture."

"It's all right. They already know," he assured her.

"Then tell me. I don't even know where we're going to live."

"Of course you do. We're moving into the beach house."

Her eyes brightened with hope. "But I thought when we couldn't close on the house, we had lost it."

He shook his head. "I just said I wasn't going to move into the house without you. I never said I was going to cancel our agreement to buy it."

She leaned back to regard him accusingly. "You knew all the time that I was coming with you."

"I hoped," he corrected her. "I would never have lived in the house without you, but I wasn't going to give it up as long as there was a chance you would change your mind. I bought the house, Connie, and it's waiting for us. All we have to do is move into it."

She looked up at him in contentment, happily contemplating the rosy future that stretched ahead of them. "It really is going to work out for us, isn't it? It scares me to think how close we came to losing it all. Just think, Eric. If Rob Nelson hadn't come by to see me today, none of this might have happened."

"It was a close call," Eric agreed.

"But wasn't it lucky that Rob happened to mention your knee?"

"Really lucky. I'm going to let him know that I owe him."

Something in Eric's bland expression alerted her, and she said in sudden suspicion, "Rob didn't just happen to come by to see me, did he? You *sent* him to tell me you had hurt your knee."

"Well, I had to do something, didn't I? I couldn't just sit here and let you slip away from me."

"You deliberately made me worry about you and feel sorry about you. Admit it."

"I won't lie to you. I sent him to tell you how much I needed you."

She regarded him with reproachful eyes. "I guess you know that was a dirty trick."

He grinned apologetically. "It was all I could think of to do."

There was an irresistible appeal in his expression that melted the last of her defenses. "It was a low, underhanded thing to do," she said, "but I sure am glad you did it."

His lips curved into a satisfied smile. "Well, it worked for Stella, didn't it?"

## Chapter 12

It was a little after ten when Connie slipped through the front door at the D'Angelo house. She tiptoed quietly down the front hallway, not wanting to alert the family. Tomorrow would be soon enough to face the difficult task of telling her parents of her decision.

She had almost reached the stairs when she heard her father's voice. "I've been waiting for you, Connie," he said.

Reluctantly she turned to face him, not ready to deal with explanations.

"I thought maybe you might have been with Eric," Sam said, watching for her reaction.

She nodded. "We were talking things over."

"Did you get everything worked out?"

"We did. Although you may not like what we've

175

decided.'' She took a deep breath and met her father's gaze steadily. ''Eric and I are getting married just as soon as we can, Pop. He has to be in Florida in less than a month, and I'm going with him. I know this is an awful time to leave you, with Mama sick and all, but right now Eric needs me more.''

''Then you ought to be with him,'' Sam said with an understanding smile. ''Eric is a good man, and he loves you.''

''But how will you manage?''

''That's not your worry. You take care of Eric, and let me take care of your mother.''

Connie sighed. ''I just don't know how I'm going to break the news to her.''

Sam put a comforting hand on her shoulder. ''Let's go upstairs and do it together. I think you're going to be surprised. I was pretty sure you and Eric were working things out this evening—and if you weren't, I realized it was time you did. I had a long talk with your mother. She sees things a lot differently now. Sometimes she can be a little selfish, but she's a good woman—and she really loves you, you know.''

They found Stella in bed watching television, but she picked up the remote and switched it off when they walked into the room. ''You're late,'' she said to Connie. ''You never called home.''

There was no sign of the querulousness that was often in her mother's voice. Still, Connie steeled herself for a difficult time. ''I've been to see Eric, Mama,'' she said. "We've been making plans. We're going to be married as soon as we can."

Stella looked as if she were about to speak, but Connie plunged on. "I know you don't want me to marry him, but I love him, Mama. And I won't be abandoning you. I'd never do that. I'll find someone to come in and look after you, and Pop says he'll help." She sat down on the bed and took her mother's hand. "I love Eric, Mama, just the way you loved Pop back when you were young. I can't turn my back on him and a lifetime of happiness. Could you have done that to Pop?"

Stella's hand gripped Connie's, and her eyes met Sam's, then came back to her daughter's. "I could never have done that," she said, and her voice quavered as she added, "My poor baby. What have I done to you? I never meant to make you suffer." Her eyes filled with tears. "Your father and I had a long talk tonight. He made me face up to how unhappy you are—and to my part in that unhappiness. I guess I've been a little afraid of my baby's leaving the nest. But your father has made me see it's not really an end— it can be a new beginning for us, once I get well."

Connie couldn't believe this was the same woman she had left that morning. Before she could comment on it, though, Sam chimed in:

"That's right. And you'll be on your feet before we know it. I'll hire a housekeeper to take care of the house and meals, and there are plenty of good people at the hospital who can help your mother with her treatment. Then we'll be able to do all those things we had to put off when we were young and raising a family—traveling, bowling, even dancing lessons.'' His eyes were sparkling, as if it were he and his wife who were planning a honeymoon, not their daughter.

Connie laughed. ''Dancing lessons! Are you sure I came home to the right house?''

Stella and Sam laughed too, but it was Stella who spoke, growing serious. ''And to the right mother, at long last.'' She hugged her daughter.

''Oh, Mama.'' Connie pulled away, searching her mother's eyes. ''You really do understand.''

''Down deep, I think I always did. I just needed to have someone talk a little sense to me.'' She smiled at Sam, then turned back to Connie. ''Something else I've always understood down deep is that Eric is a fine man and will take good care of you. He must be a fine man to have put up with me all this time!''

''I don't believe this!'' Connie laughed with delight and hugged her mother.

But Stella was suddenly her no-nonsense self again. ''What are you wasting time for?'' she said. ''Get me a pad and pencil. We have a wedding to plan.''

Connie shook her head. ''Oh, no, you don't. We're not going to do anything that will put a strain on you. We'll get married right here at the house so that you can be at the ceremony. And we won't go to any trouble. We'll have the family and Eric's parents, of course, but we'll make it quick and simple.''

Stella sat straight up in bed and looked at her daughter in horror. ''What do you mean, quick and simple? You'll do nothing of the kind. No daughter of mine is going to get married in a rushed-up excuse for a ceremony. If they have to wheel me down the aisle in this bed, I'm going to see that my only daughter has a proper wedding.''

The wedding was held in the hospital chapel. Escorted by her proud father and gowned in white lace, Connie was a radiant bride. Gena Farrell and Amanda McKinnon, wearing sky-blue chiffon, presented a lovely picture as the bride's attendants. Frankie, dashingly handsome in a white summer jacket, served enthusiastically as Eric's best man.

The most remarkable member of the wedding party, however, was Stella, who had recovered miraculously from her illness. Revitalized by her daughter's approaching wedding, she had experienced an extraordinary response to her therapy. She had also enrolled in an exercise class and shed several unwanted pounds. Wearing a flattering pink lace dress and displaying a stylish new hairdo, she made a most attractive mother of the bride when she walked triumphantly down the aisle.

Later, at the D'Angelo house, she presided with Sam over a lavish reception in honor of the happy newlyweds. Introducing Iris and Arthur Lindstrom to the many D'Angelo friends and relatives, she extolled the attractions of their Florida home. "It's a wonderful place. The Lindstroms have a lovely home on the water, with a club where they can visit with their friends whenever they like. They've invited Sam and me to stop off and see them later on in the year when we get back from our cruise to the Caribbean."

Privately she confided to Iris Lindstrom that Sam had decided to take some time off so that they could travel. With Connie married and Frankie moving into an apartment, there was no longer any reason for them to be tied down at home. They were even thinking of moving to a condominium, since Stella had never liked housework, anyhow.

Wanting to be ready for the exciting events in store for them, she had enrolled herself and Sam in a dancing class. "If I'm going to be cruising around on ships where there are all these wonderful things to do, I don't want to miss out on anything," she explained.

She also explained to each guest in turn that her daughter had married a wonderful man. Not only was he a professor at a fine college of art, but he also was a famous artist. Finally, red-faced with embarrassment, Eric took her aside. "Knock it off, Mama," he pleaded fiercely.

She brushed aside his objections and planted an af- fectionate kiss on his cheek. "It's all right, Eric. A mother has a right to be proud of her children. After all, you're my only son-in-law.''

With music and dancing and a dining table laden with platters of delicacies, the party showed signs of continuing for hours. Connie at last had to insist that they cut the five-tiered wedding cake. When the toasts had been drunk and the cake had been served, she and Eric slipped quietly away to return shortly, dressed to begin their drive to Florida.

The D'Angelo brothers had brought her little car to the front of the house, Eric's van having already been transported to their new home. Decorated with streamers and prominently marked *Just Married*, the car waited with its engine running, as if impatient for the bridal couple to begin the honeymoon.

Frankie, having checked over every last hose and screw, promised that the car was roadworthy. ''Since neither of you would have a clue as to what to do if it broke down, I've made sure it'll get you to Florida.'' He added with an affectionate but doubtful shake of his head, ''After you get there, you're on your own.''

Amid a shower of confetti, the bridal couple made a dash to the car, pausing for a final wave to their friends and family. When Frankie closed the door behind them, the D'Angelo family converged on the car to offer them an enthusiastic farewell. As Eric drove off, Stella's voice rang out clearly, ''Have a wonderful honeymoon, children. We'll all be coming to see you as soon as you get settled.''

Eric drove a few blocks amid the clamor of tin cans and a flutter of streamers before he slowed down and turned to Connie in consternation. "Did Stella say what I think she did?"

"As best I could tell, she said they were coming to Florida."

"Do you think she really means it?"

Connie sighed in resignation. "I don't doubt it at all. The entire family will be there, including the kids. I hate to tell you, Eric, but I'm afraid the D'Angelo family gatherings have just moved to Florida."

He drove in silence for several more blocks and then turned suddenly into the drive-through of a luxury hotel. Parking the car with a flourish, he turned to Connie and said, "There's no point in hurrying to get to Florida. The family will probably get there before we do, anyhow. We might as well take our time and stop off here. We ought to make the most of our honeymoon while we can."

Connie followed happily to the bridal suite with a serene confidence in her ingenious husband. Observing his skill in plotting a course through a sea of crafty in-laws, she had no doubt that their future was in good hands.